MURDER AT THE GARDEN PARTY

A 1920S HISTORICAL COZY MYSTERY - AN EVIE PARKER MYSTERY BOOK 12

SONIA PARIN

Murder at the Garden Party Copyright © 2021 Sonia Parin

No part of this publication may be reproduced in any form or by any means, without the prior written permission of the author, except in the case of brief quotations embodied in critical articles and reviews.
This is a work of fiction. Names, characters, places and incidents are the product of the author's imagination or are used fictitiously. Any resemblance to actual persons, living or dead, organizations, events or locales is entirely coincidental.
v311

ISBN: 9798473040920

CHAPTER 1

News from abroad

Halton House 1921, the drawing room

As the door to the drawing room burst open, Evie thought that if her life were to be dramatized in a play, this would be the perfect moment to set the scene for the first act.

Henrietta, the Dowager Countess of Woodridge, entered, her steps hurried, her expression jubilant as she waved a piece of paper in the air. "Evangeline. *Evangeline.*"

Before Henrietta could continue her announcement, Toodles rushed in, growling, "Give that back to me."

What followed could only be described as a squabble

as Toodles attempted to snatch the piece of paper from Henrietta and Henrietta did all she could to stop her.

Evie shifted to the edge of her chair and watched with a mixture of disbelief and apprehension as a respected member of the British peerage who had sat down to afternoon tea with the Queen, and her granny, a woman of substantial wealth and impeccable social standing, danced around and came close to crashing against the furniture.

Evie considered intervening. However, she hesitated, thinking they would surely come to their senses and realize she wasn't alone.

Glancing at the young woman sitting opposite her, Evie saw her looking down at her hands, evidently choosing to ignore the scene either out of politeness, supreme discretion or awkward embarrassment. Any one of those reasons, of course, had earned the young woman top marks.

"My lady."

Turning back to the chaotic scene, Evie saw Edgar, her butler, supporting himself against the door, his chest rising and falling in quick succession.

"Edgar?" Was he suffering an attack?

Evie rose out of her chair only to sink down again when, stopping to catch his breath, he managed to say, "My lady, I tried to stop them." He gasped in a breath before continuing, "But they were too quick, even for me." Another gasp and a hard swallow followed. "My apologies."

Toodles' voice drowned out her butler's apology. "Oh, for heaven's sake. Have it your way." Toodles stepped back but the moment Henrietta let her guard down, Toodles lunged forward and tried to snatch the piece of paper from her again.

"Aha! I knew you would try to trick me." Henrietta stretched her arm out and stepped back, using her umbrella to ward off another attempt. "You shall have to get past *The Persuader.*"

Evie closed her eyes. Henrietta had named her umbrella?

With a huff, Toodles once again stepped back. This time, she crossed her arms. "Very well. You have the stage. I won't stop you from making a fool of yourself."

Satisfied, Henrietta turned to Evie and straightened into her trademark imperial pose of lifted chin and supreme confidence, the childish taunts of moments before forgotten as she once again became the esteemed Dowager Countess of Woodridge.

"Evangeline, news about your upcoming nuptials has crossed the ocean." Giving her a brilliant smile, Henrietta waved the piece of paper with a flourish.

"Henrietta, what on earth are you talking about?" Evie asked. Despite everyone's expectations, she and Tom had not set a date yet. Indeed, they refused to be catapulted into marriage.

"There is no other option. You must marry posthaste. *Everyone* knows." Henrietta stepped forward and presented her with what turned out to be a newspaper clipping.

Instead of taking the piece of paper, Evie turned to the young woman sitting primly on a chair opposite her. "Please excuse me for a moment."

Rising to her feet, Evie spread her hands out and

herded her granny and the dowager toward the door. "Ladies. Could we please continue this conversation at a later time?"

"But this cannot wait, Evangeline. Look! You caught the bouquet."

She had indeed caught Caro's bouquet. Or, rather, the bouquet had hit her on the head and she had just managed to grab hold of it. But how had the photograph appeared in a New York newspaper?

"They will be swarming Halton House," Henrietta declared.

"They?"

"Your compatriots. The photographers and journalists are headed this way as we speak. There is a race to see who can capture the first images of you, no doubt in a compromising situation. You should warn Tom."

Nodding and smiling, Evie continued herding them toward the door. "Henrietta, I will do that as soon as I have a moment to spare."

Henrietta turned to Toodles. "See, all is well. Evangeline will now be prepared. To think, you wished to keep this from her. I've never heard such nonsense."

Walking away, their conversation became quite amicable as they discussed what they would do for the rest of the day.

Evie shook her head and stepped back, allowing Edgar to close the drawing room door.

Turning, Evie smiled. "My apologies." She walked back to her chair and sat down. "Now, where were we?" Drawing a blank, Evie searched her mind and encountered a barrage of confusion. Pushing her way past it all, she recalled the conversation they'd been having. "Oh, yes. How do you deal with constant interruptions?"

The young woman looked confused. "Begging your pardon, milady. Are you asking for advice?"

It took a moment for Evie to process what the young woman had just said. "Oh, I see. No, I believe I am beyond help." Avoiding further confusion, Evie clarified, "This is not exactly a run of the mill type of household. The position will require you to navigate obstacles and difficulties, none of which I can actually warn you about because I never really know what will happen next. Some people might think my life is quite predictable, but I can assure you it is not." Evie closed her eyes for a moment. Drawing in a deep breath, she smiled. "Never mind all that. The role requires expediency and thoroughness. No stone left unturned has become my new motto." She nodded. "I would also expect the utmost discretion, of course, and supreme diligence. Which I suppose is the same as thoroughness. Or is it?"

Eliza Barton gave a firm nod. "I shall endeavor to excel at both, milady."

CHAPTER 2

Later that day...

*E*vie walked into the library where she knew she would find Tom Winchester hiding. He had been doing a great deal of that since her lady's maid, Caro, had married Detective Evans, or rather, Lord Evans, making Caro the new Lady Evans.

Such a happy day, Evie reminisced. The entire village had attended the nuptials at the parish church and the Halton House gates had been thrown open for all to attend a wedding breakfast.

The cook, Mrs. Horace, had performed miracles, spending days ahead of the wedding to prepare food for everyone. While the rest of the servants had insisted they needed to play a role. Thankfully, Edgar, who had equipped himself with a whistle, had displayed an extraordinary talent for regimental organization, commandeering everyone into performing the task of setting up tables, chairs and tents on the grounds and organizing everything in time to then attend the wedding.

This hadn't been just anyone's wedding. Caro was one of their own. So, Evie had engaged the services of a dozen footmen, giving the Halton House servants the rest of the day free so they could all join in the celebrations.

Yes, indeed. It had been a joyous occasion for everyone.

However, the event had triggered a renewed effort by Henrietta who had launched an unrelenting assault, targeting everyone she knew in an effort to gain a title for Tom Winchester, so far, to no avail.

"Tom."

His head emerged from behind a wingback chair. "Is it safe?" he whispered.

"Yes, I'm quite alone. I mean, it's just me and you. Or is it you and I?" Evie brushed her fingers across her temple. "I have had quite a morning and now…" she sighed and made her way to the chair next to Tom. Sinking into its comfort, she sighed again. "I believe I have just found the right candidate for the position."

Tom's eyebrows quirked up. "You don't sound very convinced or confident."

"I'm not. I suspect she might be harboring some doubts. In fact, while she accepted the role, I fear she might have been frightened away by Henrietta and Toodles."

"Dare I ask?"

"You can ask but I won't tell you. Please, don't force me to relive the scene." She sat back and enjoyed a moment of silence, but it didn't last. "She seems like a nice young woman. I know I should have looked for someone more qualified and with more experience, but Eliza has a great yearning to improve herself. Her eyes sparkled with eagerness, something the other candidates lacked. Also, I witnessed her admirable resilience."

Tom snorted. "Let me guess, this has something to do with the episode you don't wish to talk about."

Evie hummed under her breath. "More or less."

"You're about to sigh again."

Evie drew in a long breath and tried to release the frustration she had experienced that morning. "Henrietta barged in, right in the middle of my interview with Eliza, and informed me a battalion of journalists is about to descend upon Halton House." She looked down at the small leather-bound book she held and tried to remember why she had come into the library but her thoughts strayed back to the interview. "I do hope Eliza wasn't discouraged. We need someone to be at hand to deal with our needs as they arise."

Tom laughed. "Did you explain that to her?"

"Yes, I went into great detail. Although, now that I think about it, she might have looked confused." During their recent case, they had been in desperate need of information. However, her associate, Lotte Mannering, had been busy with a case of her own and, in the end, they had been left floundering.

Evie tapped her fingers on the armrest. "If we are to succeed at this venture, we must have a reliable person to deal with the essential details."

"What does Lotte have to say about that?"

"I'm sure she will agree. That reminds me. I need to encourage her to hire a secretary for her office."

Tom chortled. "Now you want to organize Lotte Mannering? Should I take that as a warning?"

"You needn't worry, Tom. I could not have asked for a better partner. You question me when you have to and you offer support when I most need it."

Grinning, Tom rubbed his hands. "Am I about to receive a reward?"

"My acknowledgement is your reward."

The door to the library opened and Edgar walked in, his hand stretched out in front of him.

Curious, Evie and Tom leaned forward to look at him and saw that he held a leash.

"My lady, Master Holmes has just enjoyed his constitutional. I'm afraid he ran into some trouble with the head gardener."

"Oh, heavens," Evie exclaimed.

Edgar lifted his chin. "He ended up in the fish pond. The maids gave him a bath." Edgar drew in a long breath and huffed it out. "And, now, the maids are in need of a bath."

Good heavens. Evie looked down at Holmes. What had he done? He looked so innocent…

Bending down, Edgar removed the leash.

Holmes took the opportunity to press his nose against Edgar's cheek before strutting over to join Evie and Tom.

"Thank you, Edgar." Evie waited for the butler to leave before scooping Holmes up. "You mustn't give Edgar trouble. He has enough on his plate." The puppy distracted her for a moment, but she had too much on her mind to remain silent. "Poor Edgar. I have no idea how Henrietta and Toodles managed to evade him. He had to run after them."

"Did Eliza witness that?"

Evie nodded. "After that episode, I felt compelled to offer an explanation. I hope I didn't scare Eliza away. When it came down to it, I actually struggled to define her role."

"It sounds simple enough to me," Tom said. "You want a secretary to deal with anything and everything as well as the unexpected which might or might not involve pretending to be your cousin thrice removed."

Evie's eyes brightened. "Oh, I already have one of those. We'll have to think of something else for Eliza, just in case. I've sent her to the village to see Mrs. Green. Eliza has been in service for five years working as a housemaid and has only recently completed her secretarial course. I fear her wardrobe might not be up to scratch."

"That's being very generous," Tom remarked.

"No, not really. It's actually customary to outfit people when they join a household. Of course, it's usually livery or a new suit. Did you know they even get beer money?"

Surprised, Tom asked, "Is Eliza expecting beer money?"

"I doubt it." Frowning, Evie rubbed her temple. "Oh, heavens, I hope not. Truth be known, I've never really had to go through this process. Certainly not for a business enterprise."

"And, suddenly, here you are, a career woman."

Evie shrugged and intoned, "Gentlemen have their pursuits. I have mine. At least I'm not dragging you on expeditions to dig up the desert looking for mummies and Egyptian treasure. That reminds me. I wanted to talk to you about this week. I hope you've remembered I promised Caro we would be her first guests."

Tom shifted and crossed his legs. "I didn't realize she'd already returned from her honeymoon."

Oh, dear. He had forgotten… "They were due back yesterday and I'm sure she is busy getting her new household in order. I hope she doesn't fret too much about getting everything right. I will be ecstatically happy simply to see her."

He held her gaze for a moment before asking, "Are the others coming?"

"No. Caro said she still feels jittery about being Lady Evans and she wants to ease into her new role." Evie studied him for a moment and, to her relief, didn't detect any objections.

"When do we leave?" Tom asked.

Evie opened her leather-bound book and looked up the date. "Unless you have some other pressing matter, we will go there in a couple of days."

"Pressing matter?" Tom snorted. "My job is to follow you and now…" He glanced at Holmes. "I've been upstaged by a puppy."

His remark caught her by surprise. "But you gave me the puppy."

Tom smiled at her.

"Oh, your teasing is becoming quite subtle."

"And you are being incredibly considerate by asking me instead of telling me."

"I know! And I hardly recognize myself! I might be

compensating for all those letters and orders I issued the last time we were on a case. Anyway, before we leave, I'd like to make sure Eliza settles in first. I would hate for her to change her mind at the last minute. We need her."

Tom's eyebrows hitched up. "Just in case?"

"Indeed. Better to be safe than sorry. Also, there's that pesky pecking order to contend with. The world of servants can be very alienating and hierarchical. I want to make sure the others make Eliza feel right at home."

"Countess, I know I've said this before, but at some point, you must realize you can't control everything."

No, indeed. But she could try. During the course of their next investigation, whenever that might be, they were bound to experience more havoc and she wished to enjoy the certainty of knowing they could return to a harmonious environment.

Tom sat back and stretched. "I don't know about you, but I'm suddenly feeling exhausted."

"I know exactly how you feel and, to think, that was the result of one morning."

"And you have only skimmed the surface. You really should try to unburden yourself more."

Giving a pensive nod, she drawled, "True, and, to your credit, this is the most relaxed I have felt all day." Cupping her chin in her hand, she leaned forward and described the scene she had witnessed in the drawing room with greater detail. When she finished, she asked, "How do you think that photograph made its way to America?"

Tom straightened. "Are you about to open an investigation on your family? You know Henrietta will be your prime suspect."

"Right off the bat? You suspect Henrietta?"

Drumming his fingers on the armrest, Tom mused, "Perhaps you're right. She is still eager to gain a title for me. It wouldn't be any use to push us into marriage without securing the title first." Pausing, he laughed.

"Oh, do share."

"There is one stumbling block she hasn't considered yet and I'm afraid of what will happen when and if she does."

"Oh, what's that?"

Tom looked toward the windows and then toward the library door before lowering his voice to a whisper. "Even I know that in order to have a title one must be British and I still retain my American citizenship."

"Tom, I hope you're not pinning your hopes on that. Henrietta is modeling her efforts on the first Lord Astor. In case you didn't know, he was American. She is bound to investigate the matter and eventually dig up all the intricacies involved in his elevation to the peerage."

"Are you suggesting I should embrace the idea because, when push comes to shove, Henrietta will prevail?" Tom shifted again. "I suppose there's no point in putting up a fight."

Evie bit the edge of her lip. Tom would definitely change his mind once he learned about the requirements of court dress. Smiling, she pictured him in knee breeches and silk stockings…

After a moment of silent deliberation, Tom gave an insouciant shrug. "Anyhow, I fail to see what Henrietta would gain by releasing that photograph. So, she can't possibly be responsible."

"I hope you're not about to suggest Toodles is behind this. Grans seemed to be against letting me know about the photograph."

Tom smiled. "And right there is your answer."

She leaned back and thought about it. "Heavens, I believe you're right. But what would be her motive?"

"Now you're thinking like a lady detective."

She gave it some more thought and then argued, "Toodles has been pushing me into doing something useful with my time. Seeing me married again has never been her priority."

"Not that you know of."

"Well, if that is the only mystery we have to deal with at the moment, then I welcome it. After our last case, I feel we could all do with some peace and quiet and a visit to Primrose Park will provide that, I'm sure."

CHAPTER 3

Two days later...

Millicent felt torn.

She had secured the role of lady's maid only to realize nothing would ever be the same again. While she wished Caro well in her new life, she missed her the same way she might miss a sister.

The housekeeper, Mrs. Arnold, had assured her she would be too busy to notice Caro's absence since she would, no doubt, have her hands full making the role her own by doing everything the way she liked it.

"Yes, but it's no fun without Caro around to tell me off."

Millicent turned her attention to her ladyship's dressing table. She had made a few improvements and, in her opinion, they worked far better the way she had arranged everything.

Huffing out a breath, Millicent edged toward the table and put everything back the way Caro had liked it. Although, in her opinion, the scent bottles looked better on the right-hand side of the table, next to the big mirror where her ladyship stood to give a final nod of approval to her clothes, something she often did without even looking at her reflection. Millicent had only now noticed that and wondered if it meant her ladyship couldn't bear to look at the ensembles she selected for her to wear.

What would Caro, or rather, Lady Evans, think about the clothes she had chosen for her ladyship's trip? She'd have to wait until her ladyship returned. Although, Caro might quite possibly put pen to paper first. It wouldn't surprise her if she did.

The prospect of hearing from Caro and being reprimanded in a letter made her smile.

She turned just as the door opened. Millicent gaped at the young woman standing there. She was actually no older than her own twenty-five years but her wide-eyed expression gave her an air of youthful innocence.

Eliza Barton had been engaged by her ladyship as a secretary and had spent the last couple of days charming everyone with her easy manner and eagerness to fit in.

Millicent knew Caro would box her ears… well, not really, but she certainly wouldn't approve of her hesitation to like Eliza Barton.

Yet, Millicent couldn't help thinking there was something not quite right about her.

"My apologies if I startled you." The secretary gave her a shy smile and stepped inside. "Oh, may I? I'm ever so curious about this house. It is the most beautiful house I have ever seen. So many rooms, and they are all so beautifully appointed."

Millicent swept her gaze over the young woman. She gave a firm nod and declared, "There's no harm in you looking around."

Eliza gave her an apologetic smile. "Mrs. Arnold told me to find you. She said you could finish giving me the tour of the house."

Millicent knew the housekeeper had spent the last two days gradually introducing Eliza Barton to the other servants and making sure she became familiar with everything and everyone. But, with her ladyship absent, the housekeeper had turned her focus to making sure the house sparkled from top to bottom.

Eliza Barton glanced around the bedroom and then stepped inside. She walked around and stopped to admire the carvings on the bedhead and the Tiffany lamps her ladyship had brought back with her from America.

Thinking about what Caro would do in this situation, Millicent forced herself to ask, "Have you settled in?"

Eliza Barton nodded. "The room is far more than I expected."

"You'll find her ladyship quite generous." Her voice firmed. "That's not to say she can be taken advantage of. She won't forgive that." Millicent had no idea why she'd said that. In fact, her ladyship appeared to be willing to forgive just about anything and trusted her servants implicitly.

She'd heard horror stories about working in other houses where servants were mistreated and constantly yelled at by the owners of the house and even their guests.

She and Caro had often talked about their good fortune and, on occasion, had promised to behave better.

Of course, being quite opinionated, Caro had set a bad example and now she had to bite her tongue or else risk saying the first thing that came to mind. Just because Caro had been able to take such liberties didn't mean she could enjoy the same privilege without working hard to earn it.

Eliza Barton turned and gave Millicent a coy smile. "What with all the haste in preparing for her ladyship's trip and me being introduced, her ladyship forgot to tell me about her trip. Or maybe she did tell me and I simply forgot. This house is so grand. I've never seen anything like it. And I'm sure I've forgotten everyone's names... Is her ladyship traveling somewhere special?"

Millicent nibbled the edge of her lip. If her ladyship hadn't told her, then... Well, it wasn't really her place to say because it could be perceived as gossip and as her ladyship's personal maid, she really had to prove herself worthy of the position and...

Millicent tried to remember Caro's instructions.

Display a high degree of loyalty and discretion. And, above all, keep your opinions to yourself, you silly girl.

Millicent gave a firm nod. "I'm sure if her ladyship wishes you to know of her whereabouts she will contact you."

Eliza Barton blushed. "Oh, dear. I hope I didn't overstep. What with her ladyship traveling with Mr. Winchester and them not being married."

Millicent raised her chin. "That is definitely none of your concern and you should mind what you say about her ladyship in public." Smiling, she thought Caro would be very proud of her, as would Edgar when she told him, and she would tell him because, as the butler, he needed to know everything that went on in the house.

Millicent knew Caro had been much more than a lady's maid. She had been a confidante and her ladyship had trusted her. In fact, Caro had been a secretary of sorts.

Turning away, she only then realized she might have Caro's job but she wouldn't be performing the same duties. That task had been given to Eliza Barton.

Did that mean her ladyship didn't fully trust her?

If she applied herself, she could show her ladyship she too could become more than a lady's maid. Millicent decided she wouldn't wait for Caro to write to her. She would put pen to paper and ask for her help. Surely, Caro would be only too happy to share some of her secrets. That way, she could gain an advantage over Eliza Barton.

Millicent's back teeth gritted.

Eliza Barton could never take Caro's place. She had been engaged to act as her ladyship's secretary, but she would never have the same warm relationship Caro had enjoyed working as her ladyship's maid and, occasionally, her cousin thrice removed.

"You have big shoes to fill and I doubt you ever will." A second later, Millicent realized she had just spoken out loud. So much for heeding Caro's advice to think before she spoke.

You silly girl.

CHAPTER 4

Lady of the manor

Primrose Park
Lord and Lady Evans' estate

"My memory must be muddled. I'm sure Caro said Detective Evans had been looking for a cottage near Halton House. Perhaps her idea of a cottage differs from what I imagine it to be. Then again, Newport cottages are actually huge mansions. I guess I hadn't really given it much thought although the name itself, Primrose Park, alludes to something grand."

Tom held the passenger door open for Evie. "I'm not an expert on architecture but that looks like a Georgian house. Or rather, a mansion."

"I'm sure you're right about it being Georgian. It's really quite beautiful and I hope Caro's poor description doesn't mean she feels uncomfortable living here. Heavens, I'm so nervous for her. She looked overjoyed at her wedding. I would hate for anything to go wrong."

"You're clucking like a mother hen."

Evie grinned. "I believe I am. Please stop me if I say something silly. Caro entertained too many doubts and I don't want to spoil this for her."

As Caro's first guests, Evie felt they could help her former lady's maid ease into the role of lady of the… Well, until a moment ago, it had been lady of the house. Clearly, Lady Evans was lady of the manor.

The front door opened just as Evie emerged from the motor car.

Caro stepped out onto the portico entrance, her lips stretched into a wide smile. She suddenly stopped and stood by the door, her hands clasped in front of her. She held the pose for a moment and then, flapping her arms, she rushed toward them.

"Lady Woodridge and Mr. Winchester. You're here. My goodness. I've been looking out the window all morning."

Evie smiled at Caro's formal greeting. "Lady Evans."

"Caro," Tom said. "I hope you're not going to make this awkward for us. It's Evie and Tom."

Caro hesitated and then gasped. "My heavens. I've been practicing all morning. I even stood in front of a mirror and I still got it wrong." She leaned forward and whispered. "I have a footman. I told him to stand back for a moment because I didn't want to overwhelm you with all the changes in my circumstances."

"Well, that's a relief." Laughing, Tom gave her a wide smile. "For a moment I thought I would have to lug all the luggage inside myself."

Caro looked over her shoulder and a footman emerged from the house. Turning back, she looked rather worried. "Do I tell him to get the luggage or do I assume he knows why he came out? I knew precisely what I was going to say. At least, I did this morning, but now I can't remember."

"He looks quite eager to get the luggage." Tom nodded and stepped aside.

Caro gestured toward the house. "Welcome to Primrose Park."

They made their way to the entrance, expressing their admiration for the house and the surrounding park.

As they entered the house, Tom and Evie noticed another footman standing by the door.

Caro gave them an impish smile. "I suppose you've noticed there are two of them and I hardly know what to do with them. Henry is determined to keep things as they have always been. Although, he didn't seem to mind me telling the footmen they didn't have to wear the powdered wigs."

"Powdered wigs?"

"The previous Lord Evans insisted they wear them for dinner. Now I regret telling them they didn't have to wear them because they appear to have one less task to perform. You see, those wigs have to be powdered every time they're worn. I saw them polishing the silver this morning. The same silver they polished the day before."

"Did the previous Lord Evans entertain?" Evie thought that would justify having two footmen. Also, to her knowledge, the only footmen she knew who were still expected to wear powdered wigs were those employed by Lady Astor and, of course, Buckingham Palace, but only for formal occasions.

"He entertained on a regular basis. He had a lot of friends from his days in the army."

"I'm sure you'll be keeping them busy soon," Evie assured her as she cast an admiring glance at the paintings adorning the hall.

Caro's smile faded. "I suppose you're wondering about the paintings."

Tom slipped his hands inside his pockets and whistled. "You have quite a collection."

"Yes." Caro sounded worried. "You might as well know Henry didn't find a cottage near Halton House."

Tom smiled. "We gathered as much."

"So, we moved into the house he inherited. The Dowager Lady Evans insisted. Actually, she also insists I call her Mamma." Caro grinned. "I've tried and tried but I keep blushing. She's quite lovely and surprisingly down to earth."

Had Caro forgotten they had met the Dowager, Lady Evans, at the wedding?

"Anyhow, the house came with all these paintings." Lowering her voice, she added, "They're his ancestors and I can't shake off the feeling they disapprove of me."

Evie laughed. "I still feel the same way at Halton House."

Caro's eyes widened. "Isn't it strange. When Henry first told me he was a baron, I didn't think much of it. Well, I did when I realized what it would mean to me. What I mean is that a baron is not exactly like a duke or an earl. But the title goes back a long way. I didn't realize barons could be quite so illustrious. Some of them sit in Parliament—" Caro broke off. "As you can see, I'm still in awe of it all. But never mind all that. The drawing room is this way." Caro stepped forward only to stop. "I just realized you might want to freshen up after motoring here."

As the footman took their coats, Evie wanted to tell her to take a deep breath and just relax but she'd been in a similar situation when she had first married the Earl of Woodridge. Only time, patience and a lot of practice would get Caro through this.

"It was actually an easy drive here. We're practically neighbors. So, it doesn't really matter about Henry not finding a cottage." Evie remembered Detective Evans' original idea had been to find somewhere nearby so Caro wouldn't feel completely isolated.

Caro looked uncertain. "So… Do you wish to go through to the drawing room or to freshen up? Should I even give you a choice?"

"A cup of tea first would be lovely and then I'd love to stretch my legs and see the rest of the estate and you can tell us all about your new neighbors."

The spark in Caro's eyes faded. "Mamma assures me I'll meet them all soon enough."

A walk in the park

When Evie had suggested a walk around the estate, she hadn't expected to traverse the full length in one day. However, Caro became caught up telling them all about her honeymoon and lost track of time.

"And then, would you believe it, on our return home, we had an afternoon tour of Blenheim Palace. The housekeeper recognized Henry and she showed us through the palace." Caro lowered her voice to say, "He's actually been there as a guest. Anyhow, the duke and duchess were not home. Oh, but I'm ever so glad they weren't. I would have been far too nervous to meet them."

Evie didn't want to spoil the tale by telling her the duchess had already moved out of the palace to focus on her divorce proceedings and her new life.

Caro continued. "Far too soon, we were back. I mean, of course, I'm happy to be here but I can't remember a time when I enjoyed myself so much. Unfortunately, soon after our return, Henry received a telephone call and needed to leave straightaway."

Evie lagged behind a few steps. Noticing this, Caro said, "The horse and carriage are kept in pristine condition. I should have suggested going around in that. It's quite pleasant."

Evie stopped to remove a pebble from her shoe. "Oh, but then I would not have been able to stretch my legs." She straightened and glanced around. "Are we anywhere near the dower house?" Caro had mentioned it before they'd set out and Evie hoped she would suggest stopping for a rest.

"It's just beyond that slope," Caro signaled.

Tom cupped Evie's elbow. "Fresh country air. There's nothing quite so invigorating."

Caro gave them a worried look. "You might as well know… when I married Henry, I did not just become Lady Evans. I… I also became part of the landed gentry."

Tom smiled. "That explains the vast landscape we have just traveled across."

Caro looked over her shoulder. "We have walked further than I'd planned. I suppose we could go to the dower house and I'll telephone for the carriage. I know it sounds antiquated but it really is a lot of fun. Henry says he will organize the purchase of a motor car soon and, since I put my foot down at the idea of having a chauffeur, he has been giving me lessons."

"Countess?" Tom prompted.

Evie winced as she felt another pebble in her shoe. "Oh, yes. The carriage ride sounds wonderfully diverting."

Caro assured her, "It will only take Phillips a few minutes to get there. He's the estate agent."

Evie pictured horses galloping at full speed. "Does he enjoy speeding in the carriage?"

"Oh, no. He'll take the shortcut."

Evie gulped. "There's a shortcut?"

"Yes, I would have suggested taking it, but you seemed intent on seeing the park. If we'd headed in the opposite direction, we would have come across several cottages. Perhaps next time."

"I think the Countess would have been thrilled to find even a hermit's cave with a rock to sit on."

Caro's head lowered. "I believe my mother is still gaping with astonishment and disbelief at my changed circumstances and now my oldest brother has abandoned his printer's apprenticeship and, with Henry's help, he has joined the police force to fight crime." Caro drew in a deep breath. "I can scarcely believe it myself. He wishes to become a detective."

Evie took in the view from the top of the slope. "Caro, I don't mean to alarm you but we have reached the top of the slope and I don't see any sign of the dower house."

"Oh, it's just beyond those trees."

"Countess, would you like me to carry you the rest of the way?"

"Don't be silly. I can manage, I'm sure. Let's please walk at a more sedate pace."

"You want us to walk even slower?" Tom turned to Caro. "After our last case, the Countess has been slowing down and even has Edgar taking Holmes for his walks."

"I noticed you didn't bring him with you," Caro observed.

Evie shrugged. "He's going through a naughty phase so we thought it would be best to leave him behind. Trust me. Your cushions would not have been safe."

"I do hope Millicent is looking after you."

"Yes, she's doing a splendid job." Thinking Caro might take this to mean Millicent was doing a better job than she had ever done, Evie explained, "I mean, she's good but she is still finding her way around. She's trying very hard.

I'm sure, in time, she will develop her own way of doing things."

"If I know Millicent, she will bide her time before she changes everything to suit her. In fact, I wouldn't be surprised if you return to Halton House and find your bed on the opposite side of the room." Brightening, Caro waved. "There's Mamma. She's feeding her chickens. Did I mention she keeps chickens? As I said, she's down to earth."

In case Caro had really forgotten they had already met her, Evie reminded her. "And we already knew she kept chickens. I think it's quaint."

Caro's cheeks turned a shade of beetroot.

"Caro?"

She huffed out a breath. "Did I also happen to mention she paints and draws?"

"Heavens. She's quite accomplished." Caro didn't seem to be impressed. "Please tell me this is not another bout of inadequacy."

Caro hesitated but after a moment, she said, "I admit I'm still battling with that particular demon. I... I simply have reservations and I'm not sure what to do with them. You see, the dowager paints... *nudes*."

Smiling, Evie assured her, "There's nothing wrong with that."

Caro looked shocked. "Male nudes with no fig leaves? I nearly had a heart attack when she invited my mother over for afternoon tea. Sometimes, the dowager displays her drawings and paintings in the drawing room."

Evie and Tom exchanged a look that was a confusion

of concern and amusement. "And did she?" they both asked.

"Oh, no. But she might have. Even now, I'm not sure what we'll walk into." She lowered her voice. "I'm hoping she'll suggest having tea outside. But if she doesn't, I do hope you won't be too shocked. The first time, I didn't know where to look and, worse, I couldn't stop looking."

Evie tried to change the subject. "Is that a church spire I see beyond the house?"

"Yes, she lives on the edge of the village."

"And is that the boundary of the estate?"

"Oh, yes. Although, technically speaking, the village belongs to the estate. I never gave it any thought before, but this is how the large estates make their living." Caro glanced at Evie. "As you can see, I do have a lot to get used to."

They found the Dowager Lady Evans, surrounded by her chickens and clucking as she fed them. Tall and slim, she wore light country tweeds and sensible shoes and had smiling eyes that appeared to hide a wealth of experience and a great deal of amusement.

After exchanging pleasantries, the dowager said, "I've come out here to escape the callers. It seems word has spread about your visitor, Caro, and they all want to know about her. I wouldn't be surprised if they are beating a path to your doorstep as we speak. Mrs. Higgins will insist you attend her garden party now."

"Mamma." Caro blushed. "I hope we've come in time for tea." Belatedly, Caro seemed to remember the nude drawings. "It's such a lovely day. We could have it out here."

"You have a beautiful garden, Lady Evans."

"Thank you and please call me Louisa." The dowager looked at Tom. Tilting her head, she subjected him to a thorough, measuring scrutiny.

"Caro tells me you'll be staying for a few days." Louisa gave a determined nod. "I should like to paint you, Mr. Winchester." Glancing at Evie, she added, "I hope you won't mind if I borrow him." Appearing to forget Caro's suggestion that they have tea outside, she turned and led the way into the house.

"Countess," Tom whispered in an urgent tone.

Ignoring him, Evie looked around the pretty garden and found herself enjoying their visit. For once, they were not rushing around suspecting people of committing heinous crimes.

Evie complimented the dowager. "You have beautiful chickens, Louisa. Do you ever draw them?"

"Oh, heavens, no. They have too many feathers. I don't like anything to stand between me and my subject."

Behind her, Tom groaned.

CHAPTER 5

The rigors of afternoon tea

*A*s they walked into the drawing room, Caro nearly tripped over her own two feet. Recovering, she rushed to a table and repositioned a vase.

Evie assumed Caro had seen the vase teetering and had wanted to rescue it. However, when Evie sat down, she understood why Caro had moved it.

Directly in front of her sat an easel with a painting of a male nude and Caro's strategic placing of the vase covered the lower part.

Not quite satisfied with the camouflage, Caro moved a lamp and placed it next to the vase.

Tom walked in and, seeing the painting, he stilled. Without taking his eyes off the picture, he edged toward Evie and sat down almost as if in a trance. Snapping out of it, he glanced at Evie who looked away to hide her smile.

Caro sat in a chair opposite them with her back to the painting and adjusted her hat to serve as yet another shield against the male nude *sans* fig leaf.

Evie knew she should comment on the room or the lovely day or something, but she drew a blank.

Digging deeper, she asked Caro about the garden party the dowager had mentioned.

When Caro hesitated, Louisa answered for her, "The garden party is an annual event and Mrs. Higgins hopes to, once again, delight everyone with her beautiful blooms. In reality, Mrs. Higgins is trying to impress Lord Melville. She's set her sights on his son and is quite determined to see her daughter married to him. I'm surprised Caro doesn't want to go. It should be quite entertaining." Reaching for a little bell, she rang it.

Thinking Caro's reluctance to talk about it had to do with being shy about mingling with the local gentry so soon after becoming Lady Evans, Evie asked, "When is the garden party?"

Caro looked askance. She was either reluctant or unwilling to talk about the event.

Glancing at Caro, Louisa answered, "Day after tomorrow."

"Caro, will you go if we come along?" Evie offered.

Caro's expression froze. Evie would almost say she looked cornered. Her lips moved but no words came out. Evie imagined her trying to search for an excuse or perhaps an explanation.

Louisa once again came to Caro's rescue. As she spoke,

she pinned her attention on Tom. "Arriving at the garden party with Lady Woodridge! That would be quite a coup for Caro. It's settled. You must all go. What do you think, Tom?"

He cleared his throat and sounded distracted when he spoke. "By all means, absolutely."

Louisa continued to study Tom but she directed her remark at Evie. "Caro's been telling me about your endeavors. A lady detective. I'm impressed. It must be very exciting to solve murder cases. Henry never talks about it but I imagine his way of doing things is quite boring. He has rules to follow and superiors to answer to. While you would be able to take more liberties."

A maid entered the drawing room and set a tray on a table. Thanking her, Louisa poured everyone a cup of tea. As she handed a cup to Caro, Tom whispered, "That's what we need now. A murder case to keep us busy."

"Too busy to pose for your painting?" Evie whispered back. "Heavens, we couldn't have that."

After their interesting visit with the Dowager Lady Evans, they returned to Primrose Park in the carriage Caro had organized.

At the first opportunity, Tom stated, "I will not."

Evie pretended she hadn't heard him.

"In case I didn't make myself clear," he insisted, "I'm prepared to stage a murder so we will definitely be too busy for me to pose *without my feathers* for the dowager."

This caught the attention of the estate agent who turned to glance at Tom.

"About this garden party, Caro. I think it will be a perfect opportunity for you. You have only lived here for a few days and I'm sure there are many people you need to meet. They're bound to be there."

"That's what I'm afraid of," Caro murmured. "My entire life in service has been an education. I realize that now. In a sense, I have an advantage. I know how the other half think. Just because I have a title doesn't mean I will be accepted."

"But you're already receiving invitations. That's an excellent sign."

Caro snorted. "A sign of curiosity. A part of me thinks they are going to use the opportunity to mount a case against me and justify snubbing me in future. In any case, I suspect Mamma had a hand in organizing the invitation."

While Evie understood the social barriers Caro faced were far greater than anything she had experienced, Evie tried to make light of her concerns. "Dear Caro, when I first arrived in England, we didn't know a single soul. We stayed at the grandest hotel and every day we witnessed everyone's excited anticipation over attending house parties and balls. For weeks, we hovered in the periphery of society, without a single hint of ever being included."

"But then you attended the Duke of Hetherington's house party," Caro chirped.

Yes, indeed, Evie thought. And that's where she had first met Caro.

Evie nodded. "My mother worked very hard to get

that invitation. And, as you know, the rest is history. Despite the duke's friendship and my eventual marriage to Nicholas, it still took time to be accepted. And even now, I'm sure there are many people who'd prefer to snub me. However, it's too late because they don't know what the consequences will be. I promise you will find people who'll appreciate your fine qualities and overlook what others might think of as shortcomings."

When they arrived at Primrose Park, Evie urged Caro, "Act as if you already belong." She gave Caro an encouraging smile. "When will you be presented?"

"Presented?" Tom asked.

Evie explained, "As the new Lady Evans, Caro needs to be presented at court. It's tradition."

Tom chortled. "Going by Caro's groan, it sounds like she does not wish to be presented."

Rolling her eyes at him, Evie turned her attention back to Caro. "I take it Louisa will sponsor you. If not, I will be only too happy to do it."

"Luckily, I have just missed this year's presentation. So, I won't have to worry about it just yet."

As they walked into the drawing room, Caro blushed and repeated herself, this time sounding out the vowels more clearly.

"Oh, I see." Evie sat down. "You are self-conscious. In case you hadn't noticed, I speak with an accent."

"I'm sure it's an upper crust American accent."

"Caro, we are a nation of accents." Evie stood up. "It's settled. We have the garden party to look forward to. Lead me to your wardrobe. We must select the right gown for you to wear. I'm sure Tom will be only too happy to spend some time in the library."

Tom nodded. "I will make it my new hiding place."

∼

As they rummaged through Caro's wardrobe, Evie asked her about Mrs. Higgins.

Caro held up a dress for inspection. "Henry tells me her husband is involved in the importation of goods."

"I see. He's in trade and, even now, that's still looked on with disapproval."

"Yes, but the way Mr. Higgins lives you wouldn't know he was in trade. He hunts and shoots and spends most of his time here, but he does travel into town. I'm thinking he carries out his business by stealth."

"That's definitely one way of doing it." And that made Evie wonder about Tom. She knew he had no money troubles and she also knew her brother had a great deal to do with managing Tom's investments. As to what he invested in, she had no idea. What did they ever really know about people, even those one assumed to know very well?

"Any one of these dresses will be perfect. Now, what about a hat?"

∼

Meanwhile...
Back at Halton House

. . .

Millicent snatched her apron off, bundled it up and, looking around for a hiding place, shoved it inside a vase. Straightening her dress, she hurried down the stairs just as the front door closed. Edging toward a window, she peered out and saw Eliza Barton walking along the drive and heading toward the gates.

"The cheek. She used the front door." She had no choice. "I shall have to follow her and be discreet about it."

As Millicent moved toward the door, she heard a soft growl coming from the library. Hesitating, she turned.

The growl continued.

With a quick glance out the window, she decided she could hurry her pace to catch up to the secretary. But first, she needed to investigate the source of the growling.

Rushing to the library, she looked in and saw Holmes doing battle with a cushion. "No," she chastised. "You naughty puppy. Put that cushion down."

Holmes stilled and looked at her with his huge puppy eyes.

A moment passed and he resumed his growling. With a determined shake of his head, the stuffing came out of the cushion.

Millicent rushed in and separated the puppy from the now mangled cushion. Or, at least, she tried to. After a determined struggle, she freed the cushion from Holmes' clutches and scooped up the small dog. "You'll have to come with me." Grabbing the ruined cushion, she made her way out of the library, hiding the evidence in a large porcelain vase sitting by the door.

Millicent rushed out of the house and quickened her steps, in no time closing the gap.

She had spent the day keeping an eye on Eliza Barton. Twice, she had found the secretary in places she should not have been in.

In one instance, she had found Eliza standing by a desk and Millicent could have sworn Eliza had just closed a drawer.

After the secretary had made her way out through another door, Millicent had made a point of scrutinizing the contents on the desk. Everything had appeared to be in its place.

Half an hour later, she had walked into her ladyship's room and had found Eliza there. The chain on the wardrobe key had been dangling, suggesting it had just been handled.

Eliza had provided a ready explanation, saying she had wanted to memorize everything in her ladyship's room just in case her ladyship ever asked her to get something.

Millicent had assured her that if her ladyship ever wanted anything, she would ring for her because, after all, she was her ladyship's maid.

"She's up to something, Holmes. And I aim to get to the bottom of it."

CHAPTER 6

The garden party

Two days later, Primrose Park

𝒜s much as she was enjoying her visit, Evie took comfort in knowing she had left Halton House in good hands and would be returning to a harmonious household.

While she hadn't given the journalists and photographers beating a path to her door a moment's thought, she hoped they would be away from Halton House long enough for the journalists to lose interest.

After her recent experience with a chaotic household, she knew one only required a little patience to overcome chaos. However, Tom had made a valid point. She couldn't control everything or everyone. Least of all… Tom Winchester.

"Well, that's settled it. We can't go." Caro plucked her hat off and set it down beside her on the sofa. "Would you like some tea?"

Abandoning her effort to distract herself, Evie swung away from the window. "Someone must know where Tom is. He can't have disappeared." They had been ready to leave for the garden party for over an hour only to discover Tom was nowhere to be found.

Caro's footmen had been overjoyed to be charged with the task of finding Tom Winchester. After half an hour, the housemaids had been engaged to assist them. A full hour later, they had reported back saying they had searched high and low and had not been able to locate Mr. Winchester.

"Caro, could you please stop looking so pleased?"

"I'm not happy about Tom going missing…"

Evie tapped her foot. "I know what you're happy about and we will attend the garden party. Now, think. Where did we last see Tom?"

"In the library. He headed there straight after breakfast."

Evie turned back toward the window. "The motor car is not outside. I'm sure I saw it there this morning. There must be a hiding place on the estate you don't know about."

"The house was built in 1800. Henry tells me the previous foundations still remain and he suspects part of the structure was combined with the old building."

"Are you about to reveal an important fact?"

Caro tapped her chin. "Well, I know some houses used to have priest hiding holes but Henry's family has always been strictly Church of England so they would not have had need for one. However, there's always the possibility of a smuggler's hiding place." She smiled as she appeared to be entertaining a private thought. "Although, we don't live near the coast. You see, it would have made sense if we lived near the sea. If you must know, I rather like the idea of finding a hiding place and, perhaps, some long lost treasure, preferably stolen treasure. Henry's family is what you might call straight-laced."

"Apart from your secret wish to find a skeleton in Henry's closet, do you think your story is leading somewhere within the vicinity of Tom?"

"I was getting to that… I'm thinking Tom might have found a secret passage we don't know about but, of course, that doesn't explain why his motor car is missing. The footmen have spread their search to the village. Perhaps Tom went to the pub."

"Caro? I get the feeling you are employing delay tactics."

Caro grinned. "I'm sure Tom will turn up. I mean… Surely, he wouldn't come to harm."

Evie paced around the drawing room. "The servants have searched the house and the surrounding buildings from top to bottom. Is there anywhere else he might be on the estate?"

They both suddenly stilled.

Evie yelped. "You don't think Louisa had something to do with his sudden disappearance?"

Caro tried to stifle her laughter. "She wouldn't force

him but, *Mamma* does have a way about her. It's difficult to say no to *Mamma*." Blushing, Caro pressed her hands to her cheeks. "I suppose if I say it often enough, I will eventually become accustomed to calling the dowager Mamma."

"Caro. Please, focus!"

At the sound of a motor car approaching, Evie swung back toward the window. "It's Tom. At least, I think it's him."

Caro surged to her feet and joined her by the window. Before she could have a proper look, Evie picked up the hat Caro had abandoned, took hold of her arm and led her out of the house.

"You can put your hat back on, Caro. We *are* going to the garden party."

The motor car came to a stop and Tom jumped out, smiling from ear to ear.

"Tom, where have you been?" Evie demanded.

He tipped his hat back. "Isn't it obvious?"

Evie gave a frustrated shake of her head. "Yes, I can see this is not the roadster. We have been frantic with worry."

Tom apologized. "How did you think we were going to make our way to the garden party? In a carriage?"

Evie hadn't actually given any thought to it. "Where did you find it?"

He slipped his hands inside his pockets. "Countess, do you really need to ask?"

Yes, she knew Tom Winchester had his ways of procuring things he needed.

Tom continued, "We couldn't drive there in the roadster. How would it have looked if Caro rode in the dickie seat? She's supposed to be making an impression." Tom brushed his hand across the bright red bonnet. "Since you're about to ask, this is a ReVere 5 passenger touring car. Last year's model but this was short notice. Isn't she a beauty? It has a Duesenberg engine."

Evie tried to relax. So far, their visit here had been splendid and the thought of something going wrong had her on a knife's edge.

Evie couldn't help being impressed with the motor car but she still felt cross and concerned. "We had the servants looking everywhere for you. You might have let us know what you were up to."

"And spoil the surprise?"

"Surprise?" She pressed her hand to her chest. "My heart is still thumping."

"Wait until you see how she performs. That will definitely make your heart thump."

Evie shook off her frustration and cast an admiring eye over the new motor car. "Did you say it's a ReVere?"

Looking as pleased as Punch, Tom nodded. "Named after Paul Revere."

"I thought so. I hope no one else notices. How will it look when we arrive in a car named after Paul Revere?" Noticing Caro's puzzlement, Evie gave her a brief explanation.

Caro once again plucked her hat off. As she spoke, her voice hitched and filled with indignation, "Well, we obviously can't arrive in a motor car named after a man known for a midnight ride to warn about the British invasion. It would be… It would *unpatriotic*."

Realizing Caro was prepared to use any excuse to

abandon their trip, Evie took the matter in hand. "If anyone asks, please say it's a Duesenberg."

Tom looked at the motor car and then back at Evie, his expression pained. "But that would be lying. And, worse, people will think I don't know anything about motor cars."

Evie sidled up to him and lowered her voice. "I'm having a hard-enough time with Caro. She's about to dig her heels in and refuse to go."

Tom's back teeth clenched. "Countess, you ask too much of me."

Evie gave him a pleading look. "Please?"

Tom blinked. His chest rose and fell. His jaw muscles clenched. "Fine. It's a Duesenberg. I should start keeping track of these special requests you make. In years to come, we will walk into a fine establishment, voices will be lowered to a murmur and people will point me out and say *that is the man who couldn't tell the difference between a Duesenberg and a ReVere.*"

"Is this some sort of wildcatter pride or simple male pride?"

He folded his arms, pressed his lips together and shook his head. After a moment, he muttered, "There's nothing simple about male pride. Sometimes, it's all we have to hold onto." His shoulders eased down. "Fine, I'll swallow my pride."

"Thank you, Tom."

He raised an eyebrow. "And?"

Evie rolled her eyes. "And I'll be forever in your debt."

"Forever? Forever is a very long time. Does that mean you'll never *return* the favor?"

Evie glanced over her shoulder and saw Caro smiling.

Thankfully, Tom did not pursue the matter further. Although, even as he held the passenger door open for them, she thought she heard him murmuring his misgivings. However, she at least took comfort from seeing a spark of mischief in his eyes.

Caro yelped. "Oh, we can't leave just yet. I need to let the servants know they no longer need to search for Tom."

Evie pointed toward the front entrance and the two housemaids standing there. "They know." Waving her hand toward the motor car, Evie stepped aside and made sure Caro climbed in.

Lowering her head, Caro muttered, "I feel nothing good will come of being thrust into a social swirl before I'm ready."

Evie settled beside her in the back seat. "Out of curiosity, how long do you think it would take you to be ready?"

Caro shrugged. "Not long, I'm sure."

"I'm beginning to think you have something against Mrs. Higgins."

Tom settled at the driver's seat and leaned back. "Are we ready to set off and lie about the make of this vehicle or are we still discussing this?"

"Drive on, please."

They finally got on the way, with Caro giving directions.

Half an hour later, Evie remarked, "I thought you said Mrs. Higgins lived nearby."

Caro pressed her finger to her cheek and looked the

picture of innocence. "Yes. Let me think. Was it a left turn back there or a right turn?"

"Caro. Are you trying to sabotage our journey?"

"Fine." Caro crossed her arms. "I'm afraid I might have become confused. You'll have to turn around."

"Hold on to your hats, ladies. I'll have to make up for lost time. We wouldn't want to be the last to arrive. That will only draw more attention to ourselves and our fake Duesenberg."

Evie patted Caro's hand. "Please stop fretting, Caro. You'll be a smashing success. Remember, you're Lady Evans."

Caro gaped at her. Then, with a wail, she recited, "I want to be a lady in a flower shop 'stead of selling at the corner of Tottenham Court Road. But they won't take me unless I can talk more genteel."

Impressed, Evie asked, "Are you reciting from Pygmalion?"

Caro grinned. "I'm a good girl, I am."

As they continued on their journey, Caro told them about seeing George Bernard Shaw's play on her honeymoon and finding a lot in common with Eliza Doolittle.

Caro whispered, "I feel I should apologize for my behavior."

"Nonsense. These last few days have been marvelous. I'd almost forgotten what a carefree vacation felt like…"

CHAPTER 7

Higgins Manor

"Tom, your roadster would not have looked out of place here." Evie also noticed a couple of Rolls Royce and Bentley motor cars with the chauffeurs standing nearby.

Tom eased the ReVere into a space between two roadsters. "Yes, and to think we would have been here sooner if not for the fact that we drove away from the village and almost ended up in the next county."

Caro gave a dismissive shrug. "I'm not very good with directions."

The house stood on a pretty park right on the edge of the village at the opposite end from the dowager's manor house. Judging by the number of motor cars already there, they were indeed the last to arrive.

"Shall we mingle?" Evie suggested. "I'm sure Mrs.

Higgins will approach us at some point." With the event held outside, they could lose themselves among the guests. In fact, if they didn't wish to talk to anyone else, they didn't have to. In a sense, this was the perfect setting for Caro's first foray into local society.

"We're already drawing attention," Caro complained. "Everyone's turning to look at us. And, they're whispering about us, I'm sure."

"Caro, this is perfectly normal behavior. We simply smile and whisper right back."

There were two large tents set up with tables and refreshments at the edge of the lawn with the gardens beyond that. At a glance, Evie could see that the food and entertainment were quite lavish.

Evie sent her gaze sweeping across the small park. Everywhere she looked, she saw groups of guests chatting and laughing and, every now and then, looking around them. "You don't have to talk to anyone if you don't want to, Caro."

"Perhaps not today. But when I do, how will I ever remember everyone's names?" Caro headed straight for one of the tables saying, "I suppose one way of avoiding conversation would be to keep my mouth occupied with food."

Evie refrained from commenting. Given enough time, Caro would surely come to her senses. She would hate for Caro to feel she needed to change in order to fit in.

The strains of a quintet wafted around them, the music mingling with the murmured conversations. Many glances were cast their way but no one approached them.

Evie followed Tom as he scrutinized the food on offer. "What is that?" he whispered.

"Looks like beef tongue. It's quite delicious. Or you could really play it safe and have some roast legs of chicken."

"I think I'm going to follow Caro's lead and stuff my mouth full of food to stop myself from talking about the *ReVere*." He helped himself to a small plate and loaded it with chicken.

Just as he took his first bite, two men walked up and stood beside him.

"I say, is that red vehicle yours?" one of the men asked.

Tom took another bite of his chicken and nodded.

"We were just trying to identify its make. It's not British."

Tom took another bite and shrugged.

Evie smiled. "It's a Duesenberg."

"Ah. Yes, I thought so."

The other gentleman didn't look so convinced. "Are you sure about that?"

Evie gave Tom a discreet nudge but he responded by taking another bite of his chicken.

Not sure how to answer, Evie turned, looked toward the motor car and pretended to study it.

Luckily, Caro came to her rescue. Handing Evie a plate, she whispered, "You should have something to eat before it's too late and you say too much."

Evie helped herself to a sandwich and became engrossed in nibbling it.

As the two gentlemen continued discussing the motor car, all three employed the utmost discretion to move away from the table and the two curious motor enthusiasts.

When they stopped at a safe distance, Tom looked back. "I should have helped myself to a glass of champagne."

"You'll be returning to the tent at your own risk," Evie warned. "They looked quite determined to identify the vehicle and I'm not sure they would have reacted well to the news. Remember, we're here to help Caro make a good first impression. I would prefer to remain diplomatic and avoid an international incident. Some people can be extremely sensitive." She glanced toward the house. "Oh, there's a footman carrying a tray of drinks. He's headed this way. No… wait. He's been surrounded by a group of guests and…"

"I can see for myself, Countess. First you raise my hopes and then you dash them. Is this a new trait with you?"

"What can I say? Better luck next time. There are quite a few footmen carrying trays of drinks. I'm sure one of them will eventually reach us." She studied the guests and found herself intrigued by some of them. The country remained the last bastion of gentility with its traditional pursuits and interests. The glamour and wildness enjoyed by the younger generation, in her experience, had yet to spread beyond the limits of London.

"I'm surprised by some of the people here. They don't strike me as the type to enjoy garden parties."

"Not genteel enough for you?" he drawled.

"No, they just seem out of place. In fact, they remind me of Phillipa Brady's friends."

"The troublemaking bright young things?"

Evie nodded and continued to look around. Behind the area where the tents and tables had been set up, she could see the garden beds with magnificent looking blooms providing an explosion of color. Beyond, there were rows upon rows of rose bushes. As she looked away, something caught her attention. Looking back, she narrowed her gaze and focused on the area beyond the roses.

"What do you see, Countess?"

"I thought I saw someone standing in the distance. Maybe it was a gardener. I'm sure Mrs. Higgins has several of them." Although, in that moment, the person had looked like an outsider looking in.

She looked toward the spot where she thought she'd seen the person and decided it had been a woman. Yes, she thought. The woman had worn a hat.

She resumed her scrutiny of the guests, following the progress of a woman in her fifties flitting from group to group. "I'm guessing that's Mrs. Higgins, our hostess." Evie glanced at Caro and added, "I'd ask Caro to confirm it but the moment I mentioned our hostess' name, she stuffed an entire sandwich in her mouth."

Caro's cheeks turned a bright shade of red.

"Good heavens, Caro, I hope you're not choking."

Patting her chest, Caro swallowed hard and, heaving in a breath, she smiled. "It nearly went down the wrong way. Oh, dear. Mrs. Higgins is headed this way."

The woman waved a handkerchief and called out, "Lady Evans."

"Do we disperse and meet in the opposite side of the park?" Tom asked, his eyes brimming with amusement.

"I think it's too late. In any case, we were bound to encounter our hostess. That is the whole point to being here." Evie turned to Caro. "For heaven's sake. Stop looking at the ground. It's not going to open up and swallow you."

"With any luck, it might."

"How delightful," Mrs. Higgins said as she reached them. "I'm so happy you could come and you brought your guests." Her bright eyes bounced between them. She pressed her hands against her chest and appeared to be in absolute awe of their presence.

Caro made the introductions. "These are my friends, Lady Woodridge and Mr. Winchester. They were eager to see your beautiful garden and, in particular, your Higgins roses."

For someone reluctant to take the plunge into local society, Caro seemed to know precisely what to say to their hostess.

As Mrs. Higgins launched into an excited monolog about her garden, her words spilled out with such haste it became clear she did not require any input other than nods of appreciation from her audience.

Evie realized Caro had employed a most effective conversational tool, complimenting Mrs. Higgins on something she was clearly passionate about and getting her to do all the talking.

However, just as she burst into an intricate description of her Higgins Rose and the many awards she had won for it, a footman approached and delivered a whispered message which appeared to strike Mrs. Higgins like a blow to the head.

She barely drew breath as she excused herself and hurried away.

"I wonder what that was about?" Caro asked with interest.

"You are only curious because you wish to know if you can use the information at a future date to get rid of the woman. I'm surprised at you, Caro. Actually, I'm also in awe of your skills in getting her to do all the talking."

"I have Mamma to thank for that. In case you hadn't noticed, she's not here and that's because she can barely tolerate the woman's obsession with her roses." Caro gave her an impish smile. "When Mamma is pressed into attending a social event she can't get out of, she simply compliments the person on something or other and that always gets them talking about themselves. This is the first time I've employed the tactic." Caro looked toward the garden. "I suppose we should go look at her roses."

Evie decided she wouldn't mention seeing Mrs. Higgins headed in that direction for fear Caro might want to avoid going there.

They set down their plates of food and walked toward the flower beds.

"You didn't have any trouble identifying our hostess," Evie remarked. "I had actually assumed you hadn't met her yet."

"When Henry and I returned from our honeymoon, we visited the dowager and encountered Mrs. Higgins coming out of the house. It was rather awkward. Henry introduced us. We had a brief conversation, but Mrs.

Higgins appeared to be eager to hurry off. I understood why when we entered the drawing room. You see, Mamma has discovered a way to discourage Mrs. Higgins from visiting by displaying one of her paintings in the drawing room. Now that I think about it, that's probably why we saw a painting there when we visited." Caro looked up in thought. "Perhaps I should take up painting."

"Heavens, apart from obsessing about her roses, is she a busybody?" Evie asked.

"Not particularly. From what I understand, she simply has a habit of dropping by without an invitation. I should hate to be caught unprepared."

"And how do you feel about your other neighbors?" Evie asked as she wondered if Caro would ever come out of her shell.

"I haven't had the opportunity to form an opinion." Caro bit the edge of her lip.

"Let me guess. You don't want to give them the opportunity to form an opinion about you. Perhaps you're right in wanting to pace yourself. In time you'll settle down and find your feet." Evie glanced back at the guests and asked, "Do you recognize anyone else?"

Caro looked surprised. "Actually, yes, I think I do. There's Lord Melville." She signaled toward a group of men. "I haven't met him in person but Henry told me he is quite tall. In fact, he always stands out because he is a head taller than everyone around him."

Even from a distance, Evie could see the viscount displayed an air of superiority. Studying him for a moment, she noticed that while he had the advantage of being taller than everyone around him, he also held his head even higher and tilted back.

Evie swept her gaze around and had no trouble identifying Lord Melville's son. Also, a head taller than everyone else.

Caro confirmed it. "Yes, that's him. Henry pointed him out in the village. He's a daredevil on the road."

Impeccably dressed in a summer suit, he displayed the polished elegance of his class. Evie's acquaintance with his type made her wonder why Mrs. Higgins hoped to marry her daughter off to him. Such young men, Evie knew, led pleasure-seeking lives with no thought applied to anything that might resemble ambition.

"Do you think that's Mrs. Higgins' daughter?" Evie signaled toward the young woman speaking with the viscount's son.

Tom leaned in and murmured, "If she is Mrs. Higgins' daughter, they will make a good match. They are both quite good looking, even from a distance."

Evie studied the couple. "I'm sure he gambles too much, drinks to excess and… Well, I don't need to spell out the rest."

"Yes, but Mrs. Higgins' daughter would have a title so the rest won't matter that much."

"I've been trying to remember her name. I'm sure Mamma mentioned her." After a moment, Caro brightened. "Annabelle."

"And what about the viscount's son?" Evie asked.

"Frederick. Mamma doesn't think Mrs. Higgins will succeed in marrying her daughter off to Frederick. She didn't say why but I suspect it might have something to do with Mr. Higgins being in trade. You'd think that wouldn't matter in this day and age. Especially as so many people with titles are struggling to hold onto their estates, not to mention their way of life."

"Caro, I believe you have just taken your first step toward showing an interest in local village life."

They reached a garden bed bursting with color and stopped to admire it. Evie could identify larkspur, delphinium, snapdragons and phlox. Beyond that, there were neat rows of roses in various shades of red and pink. She was about to ask about the Higgins Rose when Tom drew her attention.

"Countess, I think we might wish to head away from the rose beds. There's some sort of commotion going on there. I can see Mrs. Higgins running around."

Evie followed the rows of roses and found Mrs. Higgins. She was hurrying from one rose bush to the other. With each step she took, her expression became more distraught.

"What on earth do you think is the matter?" Evie asked as a burst of laughter distracted her. She glanced away but Caro's gasp had her looking back.

"Did you see something, Caro?"

"Yes, look at the rose bushes in the middle. Right where Mrs. Higgins is standing."

"Oh, I don't see any roses." Evie exclaimed, "Good heavens. Do you think that's why she's in such a state?"

Just as they moved further along the path, a roar of laughter was followed by an alarmed shriek.

They all turned in time to see a woman falling off a table.

"Oh, dear." Evie saw a couple of gentlemen helping her to her feet. It took the young woman a moment to steady herself. When she succeeded, she burst out laughing.

"What on earth was she doing on the table?" Caro asked.

"I couldn't say. A moment ago, I heard laughter. But then, you drew my attention back to the roses. Perhaps she lost a bet or someone talked her into it. Oh, my goodness. I think she's trying to climb up on the table again. She might have had too much to drink."

Captivated by the scene, they almost forgot about Mrs. Higgins. However, a moment later, she rushed past them, her hands clutching her head.

"Good heavens. This has turned into complete pandemonium."

Caro reflected, "So much for worrying I might embarrass myself by saying or doing the wrong thing."

Tom drew their attention to the tallest man they had earlier identified as Lord Melville. "It seems he's had enough. He's leaving. Actually, that's a determined walk so he's storming off. And Mrs. Higgins is running after him."

Evie hummed under her breath, "That is quite a dramatic exit." She watched him head toward his motor car. She noticed the chauffeur already had the door opened for him and decided he must have been keeping an eye on his lordship.

Shifting her attention back to the woman who had taken a tumble, she saw her making yet another attempt to climb onto the table. "Oh, I do wish someone would stop her." Unfortunately, it looked as if the people around her were more interested in the entertainment she could provide.

"Does anyone else feel awkward?" Caro asked.

"Yes, I do," Evie offered. "I'm not sure I wish to linger and watch how this all unfolds. But if we leave, I will feel as though we are abandoning Mrs. Higgins."

Tom cupped her elbow and guided her toward the rose bushes. Someone had gone to a great deal of trouble to remove most of the petals from the pink roses. The rest all appeared to be intact.

"I'm guessing the pink roses are the Higgins roses. Do you think this might have been deliberate?" Evie pressed her hand to her chest. "Who would do such a thing? Mrs. Higgins has won awards for her roses. Surely, everyone must know she is passionate about them."

"I'm making a huge assumption, but her roses must be her *Achilles* heel. You might be onto something. This looks quite deliberate." Tom signaled to a group of guests. "If I had to suspect someone…"

"The bright young things?" They were an obvious target, Evie admitted, but why would they do something so senseless?

Tom nodded. "I wonder what we'd find if we searched their pockets? This is the sort of mischief they are rumored to get up to."

"Do you think they're capable of such destructive behavior?" Evie asked even though she already knew the answer. "If they are responsible, they have surely gone too far. Let's see if we can find out what the other guests are saying."

"You want to engage with the guests?" Tom asked.

"Yes."

"Without the safety of a plate of food?"

"I doubt anyone will ask you about the *ReVere* now," Evie reasoned. "They're all absorbed with the woman dancing on the table."

"Yes, I see your point." Tom tipped his hat down. "And, you are quite right. We need to get to the bottom of this delinquency."

Evie smiled. "You just want to keep busy and away from the dowager's clutches."

"Yes, that too."

CHAPTER 8

After eavesdropping on several conversations, they abandoned the idea.

"It's almost shocking. No one's talking about Mrs. Higgins' hysteria." The poor woman looked devastated but no one seemed to care.

Annabelle Higgins had her arms wrapped around her mother as she tried to console her, to no avail.

Evie felt for her. This meant a great deal to Mrs. Higgins. She imagined everyone knew about Mrs. Higgins' efforts to secure a husband for her daughter. So, not only had she suffered the humiliation of making a poor impression, but word would soon spread.

Evie puzzled over the viscount's abrupt exodus. Had he felt personally insulted by the scene? "Such sensitivity," Evie mused. "It doesn't make sense."

"Doesn't it?" Tom asked. "I assume you're referring to the viscount's departure. Maybe he knew Mrs. Higgins put on this shindig especially for him so he could be enticed into considering her daughter as a wife for his son."

"But why would he put on such an ill-mannered display for all to see? I know times are changing, but manners never go out of fashion."

Tom suggested, "Even titled gentlemen can be rough around the edges."

Evie didn't agree. "No, they can't be. Manners are instilled into them from a young age more rigidly than a regular child."

Surprised by the remark, Tom's eyebrow quirked up. "Are you about to say it's what separates a titled person from the peasants?"

"Certainly not. Especially since, in my youth, I was called a hoyden, a tomboy and, depending on the state of my clothes after clambering my way up a tree, a ragamuffin. My mother preferred to call me a hoyden above all else, and always made sure to scold me for being quite unfit for society."

"And, were you a hoyden?"

"Yes, and proud of it. I actually have Toodles to thank. She encouraged me to have opinions and express them. Thank goodness I didn't grow up in the Victorian era. I'm sure my parents would have muzzled me."

"You jest."

"No, I don't. I've heard say Consuelo Vanderbilt's mother had a brace made especially for her to stop her from slouching. It was some dreadful contraption made of metal and attached to her back and neck. She ended up developing a most upright posture."

Tom looked confused. "So... the muzzle would have given you a stiff upper lip?"

"As I said, I had a lucky escape. And, regardless of my upbringing and rebellious nature, I would never think of storming off." Looking at Mrs. Higgins, Evie pressed her hand to her throat. "She's inconsolable."

Half the guests had already departed. While the other half stood by watching the unfolding drama.

What would Mrs. Higgins do next? She was clearly in no state to salvage the garden party.

Without knowing much about her and how she normally reacted to bad news or disappointments, Evie imagined it would take a great deal for Mrs. Higgins to lose her composure as she had, which only went to show the extent of her distress. Then again, according to Caro, Mrs. Higgins had been frightened away from the dowager's house by a mere painting of a nude man.

She noticed the viscount's son had remained.

Every time Evie looked his way, she found him displaying a smug smile. The first couple of times, she thought it had been his natural expression. Indeed, she even compared his expression to the paintings she had seen of the French philosopher, Voltaire—the man with the all-knowing and perpetual smile.

However, a few glances later, she thought she caught sight of a chuckle.

"I think Frederick is enjoying the spectacle." Evie turned to say something to Caro only to find she was nowhere to be seen. "Where's Caro?"

Tom signaled toward one of the tents. "She's eating again. Perhaps all this excitement drove her to it."

"I feel I've been hard on Caro and perhaps a little pushy." Evie gave a firm nod. "Yes, she needs to do this in her own time and at her own pace." Seeing Annabelle Higgins helping her mother inside the house, Evie thought they should leave. "I suppose that takes care of any awkwardness we might have felt over leaving early."

Tom laughed. "I would have been happy to leave as soon as we arrived what with the embargo placed on me. I have a sudden urge to jump on a table and announce we are leaving in a *ReVere* motor car, just to settle the matter."

"Yes, well… Before you do something to completely throw Mrs. Higgins over the edge, we should collect Caro and head back to Primrose Park." As they turned to leave, Evie heard her name called out.

Swinging around, she saw Annabelle Higgins rushing out of the house and heading toward them.

"Lady Woodridge." Sounding slightly out of breath, the young woman introduced herself. "I'm sure you're aware of what's happened here."

Evie expressed her sympathies and assured the young woman they had enjoyed what they'd seen of the gardens.

"That's very kind of you to say so. It will make my mother quite happy to hear it. However, there is something else that would make her even happier. My mother wishes to engage your services to find the culprit."

"Pardon?"

"The roses. She is convinced someone deliberately set out to sabotage the event." Seeing her puzzlement, Annabelle Higgins explained, "My mother is aware of your interest in criminal investigations. Please say you'll do it. I'm afraid my mother will not rest easy until I can assure her you are on the case."

When Evie agreed, Miss Higgins dashed away to deliver the good news.

"Countess? Are we really on a case? Please, say yes. With the threat I have hanging over me, I'd be happy to investigate the case of a missing cat."

"Tom, you don't have to look so pleased about it. Yes, we'll look into it. Mostly because I don't wish to cause Mrs. Higgins further distress." But where would they start looking? She glanced over at the group of bright young things. "To think, we came here to relax and spend a jolly good time with Caro."

"At least you'll have a harmonious household to return to," Tom assured her.

~

Meanwhile, back at Halton House

With Holmes tucked under her arm, Millicent made her way to the dower house. She knew she would most likely be interrupting the dowager's afternoon tea, but this couldn't wait.

For the last couple of days, she had trailed after Eliza Barton every time she went to the village. Luckily, she had remained undetected. Although, there had been that one careless moment when Holmes had jumped out of her arms to chase a cat and she'd had to go chasing after him, in the process toppling over a basket of apples and ruining her shoes when the heel broke off.

Before leaving Halton House, she had monitored Eliza Barton's movements, following her to the library. When the secretary hadn't emerged from there after half an hour, she'd sent one of the housemaids in to investigate. Moments later, the housemaid had reported back saying Eliza Barton was doing research by keeping abreast of newspaper articles and identifying anything that might be of interest to her ladyship.

Annoyingly, it had sounded like a legitimate task. Regardless, she remained suspicious of the secretary.

When she reached the dower house, she went in through the back and told the butler she needed to speak with the dowager.

Bradley, Lady Henrietta's butler, looked down his nose at her. "Indeed. And you say it's an urgent matter."

Millicent huffed out a breath. "You'd better announce me or I'll barge in and don't think I won't."

"I see. Being lady's maid to her ladyship has already gone to your head."

Holmes growled.

"Do you have a leash for that beast?"

Holmes bared his teeth as Millicent snapped, "Which part of urgent didn't you understand?"

Taking a step back, the butler gave her a measuring look. "Follow me." Bradley walked into the drawing room and said, "My lady, her ladyship's maid is *demanding* to see you."

"Ah, Millicent. Just the person to adjudicate. Toodles and I have been debating whether or not to follow the trend and restyle our hair. We need to decide before Sara returns from town. She's likely to have some new gown to waltz around in. She always does and I always end up feeling rather dowdy, which is what I'm trying to prevent."

Millicent set Holmes down and straightened her skirt. "Begging your pardon, milady. But I have come on an urgent matter."

"Yes, we gathered that. Oh, have the newspaper people arrived? I've asked Bradley to keep watch for any new arrivals in the village but he refuses to do so saying it is beneath him to spy on people."

Bradley cleared his throat and appeared to be ready to defend himself but his attempt was interrupted when the dowager asked for tea to be brought in.

When he left the room, Henrietta smiled. "I'm sure he's listening in at the door. Now, what is this about?"

"It's the secretary, Eliza Barton. She's up to no good."

CHAPTER 9

Higgins Manor

"rs. Higgins wants you to investigate?" Caro took a nibble of her sandwich. "I knew she was passionate about her roses but isn't her request rather extreme?"

Evie agreed. Looking back at the group of guests still being entertained by the woman on the table, she said, "In her place, I'd be more upset about the dancing. I'm sure it's the reason for the viscount's sudden departure."

Caro agreed. "That reminds me. I tasted the punch." Fanning herself, she added, "It's rather potent."

"The punch has been spiked? Well, that explains the dancing. If the viscount was going to take exception to anything, it would be the extreme behavior of Mrs. Higgins' guest. Do you think he is the type of man to object?"

"He's the Viscount Melville in line to inherit the Earl of Sylthcombe's title. Maybe he's obsessed with propriety." Caro took another bite of her sandwich. "What if he simply grabbed hold of any excuse to leave?"

"What do you mean?"

Caro tilted her head from side to side. "I'd like to know how he feels about the prospect of Mrs. Higgins' daughter marrying his son."

Evie gave it some thought. "Are you suggesting he's not pleased with the idea. Why would he attend the garden party?"

Caro set the plate down. "To find an opportunity that would justify his disapproval." Her lips curved up into a smile. "Oh, I like that. If he came straight out and objected to the match, he would be perceived as a snob. But if Mrs. Higgins gave him a reason to object, such as giving a garden party and… and asking the wrong people…"

They both turned to look at Tom.

Evie asked, "What do you think?"

He shrugged. "I have nothing to offer but I like the idea."

"I do too. However, Mrs. Higgins is more concerned about the missing roses. Perhaps we should focus on them. I think we should start by inspecting the garden beds."

As they headed toward the scene of the crime, Evie wondered how Mrs. Higgins had found out about her interest in detective work. "My photograph appeared in the newspaper once. How did Mrs. Higgins link me to this line of work?"

Tom tipped his head back in thought. "Ah, yes. The

nightclub police raid and arrests. Are you worried word has spread and people know about you becoming a lady detective?"

"Yes, I am. Remember, I wish to remain anonymous."

"You wouldn't be able to do it for too long. Surely, people would eventually put two and two together and realize it is more than a coincidence for you to be at the scene of a murder investigation. Let me see… How many cases have there been so far?"

"Those were rare instances and… well, we were often in the wrong place at the right time, or vice versa. In any case, Lotte and I have spoken about my role. Most of the cases she takes on deal with thefts and suspicious behavior. There are also the odd cases of infidelity. In fact, she's currently working on collecting evidence against a cheating wife."

Stopping at the edge of a garden bed, they inspected it for footprints. Seeing nothing peculiar, they walked on toward the rows of rose bushes.

"It's difficult to tell. Mrs. Higgins left footprints all over the place."

Caro pointed to one shoeprint. "The heel of this one appears to be more square than the others. And look, here it is again."

"You're right. But what do we compare it to? Half the guests have already left and we couldn't possibly ask the remaining guests to please remove their shoes so we can check them against this impression. Also, if we do happen to find a match, it won't mean anything since the person could simply claim they had a wander around to admire the blooms."

Evie walked around the edge of the path.

After a moment, she retraced her steps.

"If I gave a garden party, I'd have a look around to make sure everything was to my satisfaction. We know Mrs. Higgins is proud of her roses."

Caro chirped, "She must have come out here to inspect her roses before any of the guests arrived."

Tom joined in by saying, "So, the rose petals were removed during the garden party and not before. Well, that's a start."

"Is it?" Evie frowned and looked at the remaining guests. "Most of the bright young things have left. I'd be inclined to suspect them."

Tom hummed. "Well, as you said, most of them have left but we know they travel in packs. The others are probably hovering around the village. They might even be staying at the local pub." He turned to Caro. "Is there a pub in the village? I'm afraid I didn't notice on our way through."

"Oh, yes. Henry and I had lunch there just before he left. They always have a delicious selection of game pies."

Tom's eyes brightened. "Game pies. Our favorite. Countess, unless you want to frisk everyone here for roses, I suggest we head to the village. We can have some lunch and plan our strategy."

As they drove away, Evie thought about the guests. Had the bright young things been invited by Annabelle?

During the brief conversation she'd had with Annabelle, the young woman had come across as being sensible and even quite serious. Would her circle of friends include such wild creatures?

Young, impetuous and flirtatious, they had stood out. Especially the young woman who had danced on the table. The severe hairstyles, excessive lipstick and very short skirts had made them easily identifiable. A couple of the women had worn tailored men's suits and at least one had smoked cigarettes…

No, she really couldn't picture Annabelle having anything to do with them.

Belatedly, she wished she'd been more observant, but her entire focus had been on Caro. Even now, she wondered if this could be a golden opportunity for Caro to make her mark in the district.

Closing her eyes, Evie tried to think if she'd noticed anything of interest. She knew the mind could be tricky. Even at a glance, it could capture images and retain information...

Admittedly, she hadn't really noticed the other guests who had all blended into the background in their light-colored summer clothes. Could they really jump to conclusions and assume the bright young things were responsible for stealing the rose petals?

"Countess, we're here."

When Evie didn't respond, Caro nudged her. "Oh, am I allowed to nudge you?"

"After everything we have been through? Yes, absolutely."

Caro grinned. "The first time I met the dowager, I expressed my concerns about becoming Lady Evans. Mamma dismissed them as nonsense saying I'd already been trained for the role by pretending to be Lady

Carolina Thwaites, your cousin thrice removed. But I don't recall ever taking such liberties."

Before stepping out of the motor car, Evie turned to Caro. "I suppose you haven't lived in the district long enough to know anything about the viscount's family."

"I only know what the dowager told me. Lord Melville's had a long wait to inherit and might be waiting even longer. His father, the earl, is strong as an ox. He's in his seventies but you wouldn't know it by looking at him, or so Mamma says." Caro shrugged. "Age might be like beauty in the eye of the beholder. What might seem to be old to me, might look like a spring chicken to the dowager."

Tom and Evie regarded Caro with interest.

"That's quite perceptive, Caro," Evie said.

Caro gave them a knowing smile. "I have discovered that time is one of the most significant changes in my life. I have less to do and more time to think. Perhaps I really should take up painting. Anyhow, if you really want to know more about the viscount's family, you'll need to ask the dowager."

"That's an excellent idea. We'll visit her after we go to the pub."

"Or," Tom said, "I could go to the pub and you could both visit the dowager." Seeing their blank expressions, Tom pushed out a breath. "It was worth a try."

CHAPTER 10

Meanwhile...
The Dower House - The Village of Woodridge

Millicent could hardly believe she was sitting in the drawing room and about to have tea with the Dowager Countess of Woodridge and her ladyship's grandmother who insisted on being addressed as Toodles.

Encouraged to share all her suspicions, Millicent focused on the facts and did her best to avoid wandering off the topic.

After revealing all she knew, Lady Henrietta exchanged a look of joy with Toodles.

Joy!

Bradley, the butler, entered carrying a tea tray. Seeing Millicent sitting opposite the dowager, he nearly tripped over his own feet.

"Bradley, we'll need another cup and a pen and paper, please."

Seeing his utter look of disbelief, Millicent enjoyed a moment of pure bliss. If she could be asked to sit in the dowager's presence, then she could surely prove herself useful and her ladyship would begin to take her into her confidence and perhaps even ask for her assistance in her investigations.

She might not even have the need to correspond with Caro for advice.

When Bradley retreated from the drawing room, the dowager smiled.

"Your timing is impeccable, my dear. Toodles and I were feeling at a loss. Now, tell us everything you know again. We shall write it all down and carry out an investigation. By the time Evangeline returns, we will have solved the mystery and, as they say, broken the case wide open."

Millicent told them about Eliza's suspicious behavior. "She's also keen to find out her ladyship's whereabouts."

"Why exactly does that strike you as suspicious?" Toodles asked.

Millicent found herself at a loss for words. She knew she should employ reason to explain her suspicions.

Her gaze fixed on the tea tray and, in particular, the teacake. Right then, her stomach rumbled. She remembered she hadn't had much to eat during luncheon as her attention had been on Eliza Barton's conversation with the other servants.

"It's the way she phrased it. She went on and on about Halton House being the grandest house she'd ever seen and, suddenly, she mentioned her ladyship's trip. She just slipped it in and then continued on about the house." Millicent gave a knowing nod. "She tried to trip me up so I would talk about her ladyship, I'm sure that's what she did. As if I would ever reveal anything private about her ladyship. I wouldn't, of course. Then, there's her behavior. She's ever so sweet with everyone. Oh, and innocent. She has this way of making her eyes appear larger but I can see there's something calculating about it all."

Millicent stopped to draw breath and found herself wishing they would ask her more questions. Instead, they sat and stared at her.

"You don't believe me," her voice trembled. Millicent realized they probably thought she was acting out of some sort of jealousy for the new secretary.

Had she made a mistake in coming here?

∽

The village near Primrose Park
  Outside the pub

How on earth would they find the person or persons responsible for stealing Mrs. Higgins' roses?

The challenge occupied her mind as they walked along the main street.

Tom signaled ahead to the row of motor cars crowded around the entrance to the pub. "These roadsters look like our suspects' motor cars."

"Perhaps we should think of them as people of interest," Evie suggested. "In this day and age, we could be accused of libel and taken to court for spreading rumors and wild accusations." In fact, they had only recently read about such a case.

Taking care to look as casual as possible, they all peered inside the roadsters.

Sounding disappointed, Evie said, "Not a single rose petal in sight."

Looking over his shoulder, Tom suggested, "They might have disposed of them along way."

Caro shook her head. "I kept my eye on the road and I didn't see anything."

"I'm afraid I'm no help." Evie shrugged. "During the short drive here, I had my eyes closed. What color would you say the roses were? To me, they looked pink."

"Apricot," Caro offered. "Double blooms."

"I must admit, I have no idea how we'll proceed. I suppose we could wait to see if they make a mistake and expose themselves as the culprits."

"Rose murderers," Caro muttered. "I wouldn't be surprised if this was part of some sort of mystery treasure hunt. They have probably targeted the entire county of Berkshire."

Walking into the pub, they found their suspects were the only customers. They were all huddled in a corner, their attention fixed on a young man reciting a poem.

He wore a striped pink and beige coat and a boating straw hat trimmed with tiny rosebuds. Drawing a deep breath, he twirled his thin moustache and winked at his audience.

"I wonder..." Tom mused.

"What?" When Evie's prompt failed to encourage him to share the rest of his idea, she nudged him. "Are we supposed to guess?"

He looked down at Evie as though he'd only then heard her. "My apologies, Countess. I was just wondering what it would take to entice them."

"Into doing what?"

"Into paying the dowager a visit." He smiled. "I'm sure Louisa would find them inspiring."

"You want to find a substitute? But Louisa wants to paint you."

Caro nodded. "Evie is right. *Mamma* is very particular about her sitters. She won't paint just anyone."

Crossing his arms, Tom's jaw visibly clenched and his voice lowered to a hard murmur. "I won't. You can't force me."

No, she wouldn't force him, but she could certainly have fun watching him squirm. "I think we should find a table. The question is where to sit? We must be strategic."

Tom signaled to a table in the opposite corner. "We can observe them from there and perhaps show an interest. That will give us a reason to approach them later."

Caro lifted her chin. "I think we should employ strong-arm tactics and demand that they empty their pockets."

The man finished reciting his poem, took a bow and pointed to a woman in the group.

"It seems they are taking turns." Keeping her attention on the group, Evie sat.

The young woman stood in front of the group and raised her arms as if in praise. She wore her black hair cropped into sharp angles. Her eyes were outlined with kohl, her pale face accentuated by the bright red lipstick she wore, while her arms were loaded to the elbows with ivory and ebony bangles.

"She's dressed like Nancy Cunard."

"The name sounds familiar," Tom said.

"She's the shipping heiress." And quite wild, Evie thought.

"Are you sure it's not Nancy Cunard herself?" Tom asked.

Evie shook her head. "I seem to recall reading something about her traveling to Paris and settling there."

Caro whispered, "Her pocket is bulging. If we force her to reveal the contents, we'll either find the rose petals or a flask of whiskey. Remember, I told you the punch was spiked."

As much as Evie wanted to act on the suggestion, she thought the direct approach would turn out very badly for them. "Caro, we don't exactly have the authority to force anyone into doing something they don't wish to do." Too late, Evie realized she had actually struck a chord and presented Caro with a challenge.

"My husband is a detective. I think that gives me some rights. If it doesn't, it should." Smiling, Caro added, "I'm quite prepared to assume I can do what I feel is right."

When the barkeeper approached them, they placed an order for tea.

"Tom, I thought you were keen to indulge in a game pie."

"I'm much too preoccupied for that now. There must be a way for us to find out what is inside her pocket."

The Nancy Cunard impersonator delivered a jumble

of words followed by a screeching sound. After a moment of silence, she began reciting her poem.

They sat back and listened with attention, all three puzzling over its meaning.

Studying her more closely, Evie surprised them by saying, "I think I actually recognize her. If I'm not mistaken, she is Lady Astrid McAvoy. I'm sure I've seen a photograph of her taken at the London restaurant, *The Eiffel Tower*. It's very popular with painters as well as some titled gentlemen with a keen interest in the arts."

Caro sounded outraged. "Did you say she's a lady? And she's running around looking like that and destroying other people's prized possessions? Isn't it enough to be a lady?"

Apparently not, Evie thought. For some people, leading a life of privilege was simply not enough. "We should at least try to find out how they came to be here. I'd like to know if they were invited." Belatedly, Evie realized they should have asked Annabelle Higgins.

When the barkeeper brought their tea, Evie asked if there were any rooms available. Hitching his thumb over his shoulder and signaling to the group, he informed her the pub was fully booked.

"For how long?"

"Two days."

Evie thought they would need to revise their suspicions. If the group had come here to cause havoc, they would surely want to leave as soon as possible.

When she expressed her thoughts, Caro said, "Perhaps they plan on causing more havoc." Then, with a sharp intake of breath, Caro grabbed hold of Evie's hand. "Look, she's reaching inside her pocket."

At that precise moment, Evie's gaze dropped and she looked at Lady McAvoy's shoes. They had a square heel.

Before Evie could reveal her discovery, Lady Astrid McAvoy finished her poem on a dramatic shriek, extended her arms and showered everyone with rose petals.

"There! What did I tell you?"

Overcoming her surprise, Evie said, "What do we do now?" Did they confront her or merely report back to Mrs. Higgins? Or should they proceed to the local constabulary and report the vandalism?

Caro surged to her feet and thrust an accusatory finger toward Lady Astrid McAvoy. *"Rose murderer."*

CHAPTER 11

Encore!

The village near Primrose Park
The pub

"*Rose murderer,*" Caro repeated.

The accusation echoed around the wood paneled pub.

The group of bright young things all turned to look at Caro, their gazes unblinking, their expressions stony.

To her credit, Caro remained on her feet, her face showing all signs of determination and defiance.

"Caro," Evie whispered. When that failed to draw Caro's attention, Evie gave her sleeve a discreet but urgent tug. "You might want to lower your accusatory finger."

Giving her the briefest glimpse, Caro whispered, "I feel I've committed to something, but I'm not exactly sure what."

Leaning in, Tom murmured, "Right, well... This moment calls for a unified front."

Overcoming her shock at Caro's surprising attack, Evie realized Caro had paved the way for them to question the group. There was certainly no point in employing tact when the evidence lay scattered on the floor.

She pushed back her chair and began to rise. However, before she could straighten, Lady Astrid McAvoy put her hands together and clapped.

The others joined in and the man in the striped boating suit jumped to his feet and called out, "Brava. *Bravissima.*"

Straightening, Evie stood beside Caro and suddenly felt as though she had deliberately set out to steal her thunder. Or, rather, share in the acclaim.

"What are they doing?" Caro whispered.

"Praising you. At least, I think they are." For Caro's sake, she hoped they were not about to mock her.

"But why?"

"They probably admire your courage. I certainly do."

At a signal from Lady Astrid McAvoy, the clapping and praise came to an abrupt stop.

Smiling, Lady McAvoy took a step forward, raised her hand and thrust her finger out, pointing it at Caro, as she said, "Rose murderer. Rose murderer."

The others joined in, chanting, stomping their feet on

the floor and thumping their hands on the table. "Rose murderer. Rose murderer."

Caro leaned forward and exclaimed, "You're the rose murderer."

Lady McAvoy echoed the charge, "You're the rose murderer."

Back and forth, the accusations flew, both women working themselves up into a frenzy.

"Good heavens." Evie's legs gave way and she sat down.

"What exactly are we looking at?" Tom asked.

"I'm not sure. I suspect Caro is still determined to call her out. However, I think Lady McAvoy and her companions have turned this into some sort of modern artistic performance."

"It's bizarre."

Evie mused, "They do generally have a reputation for being bizarre."

"How long do you think they can keep it up?"

The door to the pub opened and a woman stepped inside. Glancing at the scene, she shook her head and made her way to a side door. Evie assumed it led to the rooms upstairs. However, she didn't give it much thought because she suddenly found herself worrying the next person to enter would be a local villager. They would witness Caro's display and spread the word around and then Caro would never want to set foot outside her house again.

As if by mutual agreement, Tom and Evie both surged to their feet and stepped forward.

"Enough," Evie called out in a firm voice.

Lady Astrid McAvoy looked surprised.

Evie crossed her arms and tapped her foot. "Now, please explain what you were doing with those rose petals in your pocket."

Caro surged forward. "You heard. Own up to your vandalism."

"Vandalism?" Shocked, Lady McAvoy drew out the syllables for further effect while her companions echoed her shock with dramatic gasps.

Caro lifted her chin. "You pilfered those roses from Mrs. Higgins' garden."

Lady McAvoy tipped her head back and laughed. "This is precious. I never imagined our trip here would be so diverting." Losing interest, she turned and rejoined her friends.

Evie, Tom and Caro all expressed their surprise in various degrees. Caro's jaw dropped, Evie's eyes widened while Tom scowled.

All three stepped forward. Evie saw everyone at the table looking up, their amusement fading. A couple of them shifted in their seats. Lady McAvoy, however, remained impervious to the threat of a confrontation.

Caro crossed her arms. "Those roses you scattered belonged to Mrs. Higgins and don't bother denying it."

Lady McAvoy looked over her shoulder. She subjected Caro to a head to toe scrutiny, followed by a dismissive shrug. "And what of it?"

"You destroyed them."

"I did no such thing. I merely appropriated them for our poems."

"But they were not yours to take," Caro argued.

"A moment ago, I found you quite amusing." Lady

McAvoy waved Caro away. "Now, you've become tedious."

"Perhaps I can call in the local constabulary to amuse you. How would you like that?"

"The police?" Lady McAvoy scoffed. "What nonsense."

"I'll have you know we are investigating the theft of those roses and the trail led us straight to you."

Lady McAvoy snorted. "Where's your proof?"

Before Caro could point to the rose petals littering the floor, Lady McAvoy's companions scrambled to collect them and began stuffing them into their mouths.

"Stop that!" Caro ordered. "You are destroying vital evidence."

As the rose petals disappeared, Lady McAvoy raised a glass in a salute. "Cheers to you."

"We need to leave before this turns nasty," Evie whispered. Taking hold of Caro's arm, she tugged her along.

"You haven't heard the last of this," Caro threw over her shoulder.

Outside, Caro came to a stop and waved her fisted hands in the air. "I have no idea what came over me. I only know I felt an intense need to right a wrong." Caro pressed her hands to her cheeks. "My goodness. What will Henry say when I tell him?"

Evie placed her hand on Caro's shoulder. "I'm sure he'll be supportive and congratulate you on your courage. It takes a brave heart to stand up for what's right."

"Oh, my goodness. What if the barkeeper spreads the story around? I'll be the laughing stock of the village."

"Caro. I'm sure everyone will side with you. In fact, they will hail you as someone courageous and dignified enough to take action when a lesser person might have turned a blind eye."

Caro turned toward the pub. Growling, she waved a fisted hand again. "We can't let them get away with it. What if they cause more damage?" Giving a firm nod, she swung around and headed toward the motor car. "Steven and Peter. Quick, we must get back to Primrose Park."

Tom whispered, "Steven and Peter? Who are they?"

"I have no idea but I sympathize with Caro. She obviously needs to feel she is doing something."

Catching up to Caro, they climbed into the car and motored back to the house with Caro explaining, "Steven and Peter are my footmen. They're going to be our eyes and ears."

Lady Henrietta's drawing room

Had she made a mistake in coming to see the dowager? Millicent wished the earth would open up and swallow her. She'd never be able to face the dowager again.

"You probably think I've imagined it all." Millicent shifted to the edge of her chair and was about to jump to her feet and flee when Lady Henrietta spoke.

"My dear girl, I'm sure I speak for Toodles when I say we are glad you came to us with this problem. If this is the impression Eliza Barton has made on you, then there must be some truth to it. I have, on occasion, found myself taking an immediate dislike to someone who has charmed everyone else. It takes a very astute mind to detect those tiny details that give a person's real character away."

"Do you really think so, milady?"

"Absolutely. Best of all, we now have something to occupy our minds. I really don't wish to rush into getting a new hairstyle. We must fix this before it gets out of control." Henrietta reached for the teapot only to stop. "If you think she is up to something, then she must be."

"But I don't have any proof, milady."

"Not yet. Now, tell us what you saw when you followed her to the village. Where did she go?"

"To the post office. She posted a letter to her sister in London. It took some doing but I got the information from the post office girl."

"Has Eliza Barton made any telephone calls?"

"Not that I know of." Millicent gave a firm nod. "I will have to enlist the others to spy for me. Although…"

"What?" Henrietta prompted.

"Well, she has made a solid impression on everyone. They all seem to like her."

Henrietta exchanged a look with Toodles that spoke of understanding. "She is cunning. However, we can beat her at her own game. This might require you to pretend to be her friend."

CHAPTER 12

Later that evening
The drawing room, Primrose Park

With the footmen, Steven and Peter, organized into going to the village to spy on the bright young things, it was no surprise to see a housemaid walking into the drawing room to announce, "The Dowager Lady Evans."

However, the dowager's presence did come as a surprise.

Evie's gaze shot toward Tom in time to see him still.

After changing for dinner, Evie had made her way down and, walking past the dining room, had seen four place settings. She had meant to ask Caro about the fourth dinner guest but when she'd entered the drawing room, she'd only found Tom who'd explained Caro had rushed upstairs to find a book.

One thing had led to another, and she'd forgotten to mention the fourth-place setting. Now, of course, it made perfect sense.

Smiling, Evie greeted the dowager. "Louisa, how lovely to see you again."

Returning the greeting, the dowager then looked at Tom who'd curled his fingers into a death grip around his glass as if it could provide some sort of lifeline.

The edge of Louisa's lip lifted. "I suspect Caro forgot to mention I'd be coming for dinner."

Tom cleared his throat. "May I pour you a drink?"

"Yes, please. Whiskey."

"I found it." Caro rushed in and came to an abrupt stop. "Oh, Mamma."

Thanking Tom for the drink, the dowager sat down. "My presence always seems to surprise people. I wonder why that is?"

Responding to Tom's silent offer of a drink, Caro headed straight for him. Taking the glass, she downed the contents in one gulp.

"I see…" the dowager straightened her skirt. "I seem to have arrived in the middle of something interesting. Perhaps an investigation."

Caro held the glass out for Tom to refill. "H-how did you know?"

The dowager winked at Evie. Taking a sip of her drink, she shrugged. "I have a gossipy maid. She brought news of Mrs. Higgins' roses and she noticed you going into the pub and, yes, she peered through the window." Gesturing to the book Caro held, she asked, "What are you doing with *Debrett's*?"

Caro sat next to Evie. "We're curious about Lady Astrid McAvoy."

"Ah, yes. Hector McAvoy's girl." The dowager smiled to herself. "There's someone who doesn't mind being noticed."

"You know the family?" Caro sounded both surprised and relieved, since that meant their work would be made easier.

"I'm familiar with them. Once upon a time, names would crop up in conversations, mostly whispered. Now, one merely needs to turn the page of a newspaper to find that Lady so and so has been up to no good." The dowager laughed. "An old friend of mine, Lady Revesdale, has been known to say that every time she reads the headline *Peer's daughter*, she always turns to one of her own daughters to ask what they have done because they invariably have done something."

"Mamma, you were going to tell us about the McAvoy family."

"What do you want to know?"

"Anything you can tell us."

"Well, there's Hector, Lord McAvoy. He's Lady Astrid's father. He followed in his father's footsteps and married an American heiress. He actually did a lot better than his father. Celestine's fortune comes from copper mining and actually saved the leaky roof at the manor house. It's strange to think of the sort of information one picks up along the way. I'm sure I heard say the mine is located somewhere in Arizona." She looked at Evie. "Does that sound right to you?"

"I couldn't really say." Evie glanced at Tom and, to her surprise, he nodded.

"Oh, Tom seems to know." The dowager smiled at him.

Too late, Tom recognized his mistake in drawing attention to himself. He poured another drink and took a casual step away.

"But why do you want to know all this?" the dowager asked.

As Caro explained their interest in Lady McAvoy, Tom settled into a chair well out of the dowager's line of vision.

Evie smiled. Out of sight, out of mind. However, there would be no place to hide during dinner.

"Well, I'm not surprised Lady Astrid has turned into a wild child. Too much money and not enough to do. From what I hear, she's quite prominent in that bright young things set and likes to stand out. I believe she has published a book of poems. But why would she steal Mrs. Higgins roses?"

Caro gave a dismissive wave of her hand. "She used it as part of her silly performance."

"It shouldn't really surprise me," Louisa said. "It's just the sort of tomfoolery they enjoy. Although, unless the story appears in the newspapers, there's really not much point to it. Indeed, there's no reason for them to be here, so far away from the center of their world. Perhaps they're not quite finished yet."

"That's what Caro thinks. Now, her footmen are keeping watch," Evie informed her.

The dowager turned to Caro. "Oh, I was just making

conversation. Do you really expect more trouble from them?"

Caro shuddered. "I wouldn't be surprised if they terrorize the village during the night. By the way, Mamma. With the footmen busy in the village, the housemaids will have to step in and serve at dinner."

The dowager turned to Evie. "I knew Caro would be a breath of fresh air. And how exciting this is. You have been drawn into a mystery."

"I'm not sure we can call it that. Although…" Caro tapped a finger against her glass. "We don't actually know why they're here. For all we know, someone is responsible for luring them to our little village. If we drew up a list of suspicious characters, I would have no qualms about including Lord Melville. He might have had a hand in sabotaging the garden party."

The idea caught everyone's attention again.

Evie turned to the dowager. "Caro thinks the viscount disapproves of the match between his son and Mrs. Higgins' daughter, and she believes he used the opportunity to express his objections. What do you know about the viscount?"

"He is an outright snob but he pretends to be everyone's friend. His wife, on the other hand, does not bother pretending. They'll want their son to make the right choice and I doubt it will be Annabelle. While today's youth like to think they can make their own choices, there is the matter of inheritance. Young Frederick will want to please his parents."

Evie's eyebrows drew down. "If he did happen to be

against the marriage, would the viscount go to any lengths to interfere?"

The dowager asked Caro to describe the scene at the garden party again. She listened with interest and, after a moment, she said, "I doubt he has the creative mind to come up with such a stunt. Perhaps he got lucky and the bright young things just happened along at the right time."

Evie didn't care for coincidences. "I'm not sure they came here by accident or chance. In fact, I'm surprised they motored all the way out here. However, we do know they will be here for two more days. The country is not exactly their preferred milieu. I'm thinking they had a specific purpose for coming here."

"I agree." Caro declared, "Mark my word, they will get up to some sort of mischief before the sun comes up."

"Well, then we're bound to read about it in the newspapers. In this day and age, this is the sort of news that makes the front pages." The dowager smiled at Evie. "Caro could not have come up with a better entertainment for you."

CHAPTER 13

Later that evening
Primrose Park, the dining room

"We'll have to call on Mrs. Higgins tomorrow." Until that moment, Evie had been thinking how much she'd enjoyed her meal. With everything that had happened, she'd actually forgotten she had been engaged to find the rose thief. "It's not something I'm looking forward to. What if Mrs. Higgins insists on pressing charges? We no longer have proof of the theft. It will be our words against theirs. I'm afraid Mrs. Higgins will be even more upset."

"But at least she will know the identity of the persons responsible," Caro offered.

"I doubt that will be enough. We're still puzzling over the reasons for their actions. I'm sure she'll want to know why they targeted her."

Caro shook her head. "While I saw it with my own eyes, I still can't believe they ate the evidence. What sort of people are they?" In the next breath, Caro chirped, "I've just realized…" She glanced around the table and seeing that everyone had finished their dessert, she rose to her feet. "This is the first time for me… Ladies."

They all looked at Tom. As the only gentleman, he could hardly remain behind to enjoy his brandy and cigar by himself. In any case, Tom didn't smoke cigars or drink brandy.

To Evie's surprise, he did not make a move to join them.

Evie guessed he'd been looking forward to spending a few minutes away from the dowager's constant scrutiny.

"Tom," Evie smiled at him. "I'm sure Louisa and Caro won't mind if you smoke your cigar and drink your brandy in the drawing room."

"He's welcomed to join us," Caro said.

"Yes, indeed." The dowager surprised them by saying, "I might even join him. I do love the aroma of a good cigar."

Caro smiled all the way to the drawing room. Evie didn't need to look over her shoulder to see Tom dragging his feet and rolling his eyes heavenward.

Settling down on a sofa, Caro and Evie tried their best to hide their amusement.

Tom went to stand by the fireplace and accepted a cigar from one of the housemaids.

As suggested, Louisa helped herself to a cigar, prompting Caro to lean in and whisper, "Mamma grew up in an eccentric household. Before her marriage, she lived in Paris and took lessons from *French painters*. I believe that's where she acquired some of her most colorful traits. Lord Evans had a hard time convincing her to give up that life and accept his hand in marriage."

A maid walked in and stood by the door looking straight at Caro.

Caro whispered, "I've been the maid standing at the door trying to catch your attention and now, here I am…" Caro signaled to the maid who took an awkward step toward her.

When the maid found the courage, she approached. "Begging your pardon… milady."

"What is it, Mariah?"

"It's Steven and Peter. They just returned."

Both worried and excited, Caro said, "Ask them to come in."

"Milady, they're not suitably dressed."

"Never mind all that."

"Heavens," Evie whispered. "Something must have happened. You asked them to keep watch until tomorrow and the clock hasn't struck midnight."

The two footmen entered. One had mud and scratches on his face and the other had a rip on his coat sleeve.

The dowager blew out a puff of cigar smoke. "This looks interesting."

Caro pressed her hands to her cheeks. "Steven? Peter? What on earth happened to you?"

One of the footmen cleared his throat and shuffled his feet. "Milady, we were keeping watch and listening to them rambling on…"

The other footman elbowed him.

"I mean… they were reciting poetry, milady. Suddenly, they all jumped to their feet and stampeded out of the pub. They'd been drinking quite a bit so we assumed they wouldn't go far, but they did. Next thing we knew, they were taking off in their roadsters and we had to give chase in our bicycles."

Evie struggled to picture the scene. The two footmen were quite tall and well built. She had no doubt they had tried their best to keep up with the bright young things. But even the most enthusiastic pedaling would have been no match against the motor cars.

"They drove away from the village and we did our best to keep them in sight. Then, they turned. That's when we thought we'd lost them for good. We still had some catching up to do so we really pushed ourselves. But by the time we made the bend, they'd disappeared."

"We're sorry, milady." The other footman tucked his torn sleeve into place. "We came off our bicycles."

"Oh, my goodness. Did you hurt yourselves?"

Both footmen shook their heads. "Only our pride, milady. We simply couldn't keep up with them. But the lane they turned into only leads to one place."

Caro moved to the edge of her seat. "Where?"

"The viscount's estate. That was about an hour ago. It took us that long to get back here in the dark."

Thanking them for their efforts, she suggested they tend to their scratches.

"What do we do now?" Caro asked.

In Evie's opinion, without actual proof, they could only assume and reach a great many conclusions.

Tom set his unlit cigar down. "I think I should motor out there and see if I can find them."

"Absolutely not." Evie couldn't think of any other way to discourage the idea. "You're not familiar with these roads and it's pitch black out there. We can't have you going missing again."

"Again?" The dowager studied him with interest.

While Caro told the dowager about Tom's escapade, Evie reasoned with him.

Settling back in her seat, Caro asked, "Does anyone have any theories about the rose murderers? Can we assume they went to see Lord Melville or did they go there to cause some sort of mischief?"

"If that's the case, we'll hear all about it tomorrow, I'm sure. If they called on the viscount, we might have reason to believe he did have something to do with bringing them here." Although, Evie had no idea how they would come by the information.

"There is an alternative," the dowager said. "They might have gone to the fishing lodge. There's a river on the edge of the estate and, as it's far enough away from the main house, there is a lodge to accommodate anyone wishing to spend the day fishing. Frederick spends a great deal of time there. I suspect it has to do with his mother being overbearing."

"Mamma, how do you know that he stays at the lodge?"

"It's common knowledge with the poachers. Whenever he's in the country, they steer clear of that part of the river. He's been known to entertain his friends there."

"Are you actually suggesting Frederick might have

been responsible for bringing the bright young things here? And... how do you know what the poachers get up to?"

The dowager swirled the contents of her glass and then drew on her cigar. "In time, you'll come to learn news reaches you whether you want to hear it or not. I would suggest taking up some sort of interest to keep yourself entertained and above it all, but you seem to have found one already. As I've said, Henry could not have made a better choice."

Caro fanned herself. "Mamma likes to make me blush."

The dowager set her glass down. "This has been an entertaining evening. I'm sure tomorrow will come soon enough and we'll all be in an uproar about something or other."

"Mamma, I think you should spend the night here."

"Thank you, but I'm actually eager to return home. I'm sure my maid will be bursting with news. She's been known to wake me up at the oddest hour of the night on the pretext of having heard a noise only to tell me some news she forgot to share during the day. Besides, Thomson is as punctual as ever. I can hear the motor car and I don't like to keep him waiting."

Caro walked the dowager to the door, leaving Evie to witness Tom's relief.

"I swear the dowager spent the night trying to picture me under my clothes." He raked his fingers through his hair. "Something tells me this isn't over."

"What do you make of the suggestion Frederick might be responsible for bringing Lady McAvoy's group here?" Evie asked.

He shrugged. "According to Louisa, the viscount doesn't have the imagination to come up with the idea. Someone else must have organized the rose heist."

"To what end?"

Caro walked back in saying, "Mamma will telephone if she hears any news. I feel I should apologize for all this havoc. I'm sure you were both looking forward to a quiet time."

"I'm inclined to think my quiet days are well and truly over and, since I feel I still owe Mrs. Higgins a report, we need to put our heads together. Somehow, we must discover what Lady McAvoy and her entourage got up to tonight. At least, the innkeeper will be able to tell us what time they returned. That should give us an indication of how long they were away."

Caro sat down and, after a moment, flopped back in her chair. "I still think strongarm tactics will work best with them."

"We'll leave that as a last resort, shall we? For now, I do have a mystery I need to solve." Wishing to change the subject, Evie told Caro about the photograph that had appeared in a New York newspaper.

"Have you spoken with the photographer Henry hired?" Caro asked.

Evie looked at Tom. "Why didn't we think of that?"

Tom laughed. "We were too busy suspecting Henrietta and Toodles."

CHAPTER 14

Meanwhile, the next day...
Halton House

Millicent hugged Holmes close to her chest. She didn't dare set him down because every time she did, he barked and chased his tail. Right now, she needed to focus on Eliza Barton opening the door to her room.

Hiding in the room next door, Millicent had been waiting for over half an hour for the secretary to finish dressing and make her way down to the kitchen for breakfast.

Holmes whined and Millicent's stomach gave a loud rumble.

"We're a fine pair," she whispered.

The dowager and Toodles had both agreed she needed to uncover some sort of incriminatory evidence and the obvious place to look for it would be Eliza Barton's bedroom.

Millicent had spent several minutes arguing against committing such a breach of privacy, but then the dowager had drawn her focus to the ultimate prize.

"Faint heart never won fair maiden," Millicent whispered. Even now, she felt her cheeks color. When she'd argued that she didn't wish to win a fair maiden, the dowager had gone into a lengthy and complicated explanation about literal, metaphorical and loose meanings. In the end, Millicent had simply agreed to do her best.

Hearing the door next door opening, she put her finger to her lips.

Eliza Barton had a very distinct way of walking with the heels of her shoes clicking along the floorboards in rapid succession. "She scurries," Millicent whispered. Reluctantly, she acknowledged the possibility she might have acquired the trait at her previous place of employment where she might have been required to make haste.

Her hand curled around the door handle. Now, she only needed to wait and make sure Eliza didn't return. Pressing her ear to the door, she strained to hear her going down the stairs.

Finally, the way was clear for her.

"Holmes, let's get our stories straight. If anyone catches us, you heard a mouse in her room and scratched the door. Before you could damage the woodwork, I went in to investigate. Is that clear?" Despite not expecting Holmes to respond, he gave his tail a vigorous wag.

Tiptoeing out of the room, she looked down the hallway and, just to be on the safe side, she rushed to the door leading to the servants' stairs. Easing it open, she looked down the stairs and heard the sound of footsteps receding.

Hurrying back, she dashed inside the room and, ignoring her thumping heart, she looked around. The bed had been made and the clothes put away. She walked toward a small table and inspected the contents but found nothing unusual.

With her fingers trembling, she reached down and opened a drawer. Inside it, she found some paper and a fountain pen.

"That looks fancy." Digging inside her pocket, she brought out a handkerchief and used it to pick up the pen. Millicent had heard her ladyship talking about fingerprints being able to identify people and she didn't want to risk implicating herself.

Studying the fountain pen, she found two initials etched on the cap.

"P.L." Those were definitely not Eliza Barton's initials. Had she stolen it?

Putting the fountain pen back, Millicent closed the drawer and looked around the room.

"If I had something I didn't want anyone to find, where would I hide it?"

She looked under the mattress and ran her hand behind the headboard. Finding nothing, she hurried around the bed and went to stand in front of the wardrobe.

Fear of discovery had her heart thumping against her chest. While she had an excuse ready, if caught in the act, she might fall to pieces.

"Let's be quick about this." If Eliza Barton had anything to hide, Millicent thought she would find it in her luggage.

She opened the wardrobe door and, taking care not to disturb the tidy stack of clothes, she searched through them, slipping her hand between each item. When she slid her hand along the last blouse, her fingertips collided with what felt like an envelope. Slipping it out, she removed the letter and sent her eyes racing along the page, doing her best to memorize the contents.

She had what she had come for.

When she finished, she put the envelope where she had found it, stepped back, glanced around the room, and made her way out saying, "Holmes, you are such a naughty boy. Next time, leave the mouse chasing to the cats."

Primrose Park

Waking up earlier than usual, Evie dressed and then sat at her dressing table to jot down a few lines in her journal. When she'd woken up, she had made the decision to make a few notes to use as future reference.

Why hadn't she and Tom looked further than Henrietta and Toodles as suspects for the unexpected appearance of her photograph in a New York newspaper? "Perhaps because we didn't consider the matter serious enough to pursue." In her mind, she admitted, it had been just another bit of harmless mischief.

Next, she turned her thoughts to Lady McAvoy and her entourage. Why had they visited the viscount's estate? To see the viscount or his son? Or had they driven there to cause further trouble? If that was the case, they would soon hear all about it. But what if they had been accomplices, working with either the viscount or his son to publicly humiliate Mrs. Higgins?

If the viscount disapproved of the match between his son and Mrs. Higgins' daughter, Evie thought he would be motivated to act and set something in motion.

She looked up. "What about the son?"

He looked like someone who enjoyed having fun, perhaps at other people's expenses.

"That's supposition," she murmured, only to argue, "yes, but it's based on my observations of Frederick."

Evie set aside her journal and, thinking it was still too early to go down to breakfast, she penned a letter.

Dear Grans

Tom and I arrived safely and were overjoyed to find Lady Carolina Evans in fine spirits. We have now been here long enough to witness Caro's happiness in her new circumstances. She lives within easy walking distance of a quaint and tranquil village and her nearest neighbor is the most charming Louisa, Lady Evans. Tom finds her fascinating.

. . .

Hearing the sound of voices, Evie set her pen down and looked out the window.

The footmen, Steven and Peter, were riding off toward the village. They wore their country tweeds so Evie assumed they had once again been sent on a spying mission.

She watched them until they disappeared from sight and then, she resumed her letter writing.

Caro is very fortunate to be surrounded by enthusiastic and loyal servants. In the short time since her wedding, she has adapted to her new life with admirable ease. We recently attended a garden party and met some of her charming neighbors who will, no doubt, soon be gracing her dinner table. Would you believe it, Caro has expressed a desire to take up painting!

We have, so far, spent a jolly evening full of chatter and laughter and I have no doubt there will be many more, especially as Caro has surprised us with her acting abilities.

Will write more soon.

In dashing haste.

Your loving granddaughter

Birdie

She wrote a similar letter to Henrietta, once again choosing to leave out the unsavory details of the previous day. Although, she knew only too well the truth had a habit of erupting when she least expected it.

When she finished, she addressed both letters and took them down with her. The less said, the better, she insisted and thought she could always embellish the story when they returned to Halton House.

She set the letters on a tray and made her way into the dining room where she found Tom helping himself to breakfast.

"Good morning. Where's our hostess?"

"Caro was here a moment ago but she raced out saying she needed to organize something or other."

Evie picked up a plate and helped herself to some bacon and eggs. "Did she say if Louisa telephoned with news about Lady McAvoy and her circle of miscreants?"

"No news. I think that's why Caro is in a state."

"What do you mean? What sort of state?"

Tom drew out a chair for Evie and then made his way to the other side of the table. "She came in, sat down, jumped to her feet, picked up a plate, set it down, sat down again and then…" He looked up as if trying to remember the precise sequence of events. "Oh, yes. And that's when she dashed out."

"Heavens. How long ago was that?"

"About twenty minutes ago. In case you're wondering, this is my second helping."

Evie gave the matter some thought and then exclaimed, "Oh, I saw the footmen setting out. Maybe she went to organize them, but that was a while ago. I suppose something else must have held her up." Evie hoped it was nothing serious.

A maid walked in carrying a pot of coffee.

Remembering her name, Evie greeted her, "Good morning, Mariah." As the maid filled her cup, Evie asked, "Have you seen Lady Evans?"

The maid bit her lip and spoke in a soft voice, "I shouldn't really say, I'm sure I shouldn't." Mariah straightened and stepped back. "In fact, I know I shouldn't say."

Evie glanced at Tom and found him mirroring her look of surprise.

Mariah sounded just like Millicent.

The maid took several more steps back until she bumped against the sideboard. Her lips were slightly puckered up, suggesting she might be either humming or whistling a tune under her breath.

Turning her attention to her breakfast, Evie lifted the cup of coffee to her lips. She supposed all would soon be revealed.

The sound of a motor car coming to an abrupt stop made her revise her thought. "I think we're about to get some news."

Mariah rushed to the window. "It's the dowager's Bentley."

Evie considered getting up but then decided the news would reach them eventually.

"Oh," Mariah exclaimed. "Her ladyship has run outside and, Thomson, the dowager's chauffeur, has jumped out of the motor car. He's now removed his cap. He appears to be gasping for breath. How odd. I never realized driving could be so tiring. Oh, perhaps he ran to the motor in a rush to get here and is still trying to catch his breath."

Evie felt she really had no need to go to the window since Mariah seemed quite eager to give them an exact account.

"Oh, my goodness. Her ladyship looks horrified. Her

mouth is gaping open, her eyes are wide. Thomson must have revealed something truly horrendous for her to react in such a manner. She's now swung around, picked up her skirt and is running toward the front door. Any minute now, I'm sure we'll hear her footsteps thumping on the floor as she makes a mad dash in here to share the news."

They did indeed hear footsteps thumping along the entrance and heading toward them. They all turned toward the door only to hear the footsteps suddenly stop and start again… heading in the opposite direction.

Puzzled, they waited to see what would happen next, their patience was rewarded when they heard a swift and loud descent down the stairs.

Caro burst into the dining room. "Oh, dear, Evie. There you are." She pressed her hand to her chest and heaved in a big breath. "I went upstairs thinking you were still in your room." Caro approached a chair and collapsed into it. "Oh, my goodness. News…" she gulped in another breath. "News just reached me." She signaled to the window.

Evie nodded. "Yes, we know about Thomson delivering news. What's happened?"

"A woman's been murdered."

CHAPTER 15

Murder and mayhem

The dining room, Primrose Park

The drawback to receiving fresh news with scant details left them feeling flabbergasted and quite undecided as to what to do next.

With the announcement still echoing in their minds, they listened with eager attention.

Still sounding out of breath, Caro related the rest of the news, "Thomson only knows what Mamma's maid told him and the maid got the news from the maid down the street. She heard a commotion early this morning and, looking out the window, she saw a police vehicle driving through the village. A while later, she ran after a delivery boy she saw cycling from the direction the police had headed toward and he gave her the news about the murdered woman."

Caro stopped to take a sip of her coffee. When she resumed her tale, the words spilled out with such urgency, Evie felt as though they needed to spring into action. "Mamma thought I would want to know straightaway. She tried to telephone but she couldn't get a connection. Mamma's chauffeur, Thomson, said he saw the footmen, Steven and Peter, in the village. Earlier, I sent them off to see if Lady McAvoy's entourage had returned. Knowing Thomson would return to the dower house, I asked him to try and find them and tell them to remain in the village, just in case they can get more news."

"Well, this is a strange turn of events." Evie frowned and found herself puzzling over her remark. "I'm not sure why I said that. Someone has died and suddenly I'm thinking it is somehow connected to the garden party. Am I being too hasty? Actually, forget I said any of that."

Caro helped herself to some toast. "I think I should eat something. I have a feeling we will be run off our feet soon. I happen to think you are quite correct in saying there is a connection. And I'll even go so far as to say Lady McAvoy is involved."

"Tom? What do you think?"

"A woman has been murdered. That's all we know, but what does that tell us?"

Evie took a pensive sip of her coffee. "Are you proposing we analyze the little information we have?"

"You know as much as I do. We have no choice. We must theorize."

"Yes, but where to start? Oh, of course. A woman has been murdered." She turned to Caro. "This is a small village. How many people do you think live here?"

Caro made a quick calculation. "There are no more than forty people living in the village and there are probably a hundred living in the surrounding farms and estates."

"Can we assume the woman was found somewhere within the vicinity of the village?" Evie asked.

"We'll have to," Tom agreed.

"Well, then… with only forty people residing in the village, if someone is missing, someone would surely know it straightaway."

Caro thought about it for a moment and then agreed. "Unless, the woman murdered is Lady McAvoy and her friends are in a drunken daze and haven't noticed her absence."

Tom and Evie looked at her with stunned surprise.

"Oh, dear. Have I shocked you with my macabre imagination?"

"Not at all," Evie assured her. "In fact, you make a valid point. I suppose we must now decide on a course of action. Do we remain here and wait for more news or do we venture out to the village?"

Tom suggested going to the pub. "We might be able to find out if any of the guests are missing." He turned to Caro. "With Detective Evans away, there is bound to be another detective on the scene."

"Then again," Evie shrugged. "We really have no business sticking our noses in."

"Speak for yourself." Caro gave a firm nod. "I'm

married to a detective and that makes me curious by association. Besides, we are still carrying out an investigation. At least, that can be our excuse." She looked up at the maid. "Mariah, please let Mrs. Haighs know we might be late for luncheon and she should only prepare something light. Actually, tell Mrs. Haighs she shouldn't worry about preparing luncheon for us. We will call on the dowager. Her house has a clear view of the village and I'm sure she will be only too happy to feed us."

Tom nearly spilled the coffee on himself.

Buttering her toast, Caro shook her head. "I just knew something dreadful would happen. I wonder where the woman was found?" She set her butter knife down. "Oh, what if she was found on the road leading to the viscount's estate? That would be very bad for him. He would surely be a prime suspect."

"I think you might be getting ahead of yourself, Caro," Evie warned.

"Countess, do you really need to be reminded how your wild ideas have proven to be quite useful in the past?"

"Yes, I suppose it does always help to imagine all possibilities."

Caro gave a decisive nod. "We should actually contact the police and tell them what we know. They will be interested to know about Lady McAvoy's group driving out last night. Even if they were not directly involved, they might have seen something." She picked up the piece of toast only to set it down again. "Can you believe it? Someone has been murdered."

"Actually," Evie mused, "we don't really know that for

sure. It could be a case of someone going out for an early morning walk and having a heart attack."

"I'm only grateful it's not one of us." Caro looked up and searched for Mariah. "Oh, dear. Mariah, are we all here?"

The maid's brows puckered and she counted with her fingers.

They all looked at her and waited with baited breaths for the result. At one point, she seemed to hesitate. Frowning, she began counting again.

Finally, she gave a firm nod. "Yes, milady. We are all present."

"Well, that's a relief. Mariah, please go down and tell everyone about the news. They should all stay indoors. And no one should walk home alone. Ask Phillips to be ready to accompany Mrs. Haighs and Rosie when they leave." Turning to Evie, she explained, "They live in the village. We can't be too careful."

Evie could not have felt prouder of Caro. It seemed, when it really mattered, Caro knew how to take the reins.

Following Caro's lead, Evie turned her focus to her breakfast. Halfway through, she abandoned her effort. "I'm beginning to think we made a mistake in not reporting Lady McAvoy and her friends to the police. What if they are involved in this incident? If we'd spoken up, we might have prevented a death. At the very least, we might have brought them to the attention of the police."

"Hindsight," Caro murmured. "It can be quite instrumental in offering clarity but it can also be a stumbling block. There's nothing we can do about yesterday."

"Caro, when did you become so philosophical?" Evie asked.

"I'm not quite there yet. This is just the sort of remark Mamma would make. As well as my own mother. Although, she would just tell me to put the roast in the oven."

"The roast?"

"Yes, as if to say, this is what we're doing now… Cooking the roast and there's no point in thinking about the chicken we might have had instead."

"Your mother is a very wise woman, Caro."

"Anyhow, I'm actually thinking about daisy chains."

"The type you make with flowers?" Evie asked.

"Yes. I'm thinking this death is somehow connected to the garden party we attended."

"In what way?"

"I'm not sure. It's only a general observation."

Mariah gasped.

They all turned to look at her, intrigued by the gasp as well as the fact she still stood by the window.

"What is it, Mariah?"

"It's the coppers, milady. They're coming up the drive."

CHAPTER 16

The sound of tires crunching along the loose gravel had everyone shifting to the edge of their seats.

"It's definitely the coppers, milady," Mariah declared, her tone excited. "One of them just hopped off. I don't recognize him. Wait, I see another copper climbing out of the motor. He's putting his hat on and adjusting his coat. Now he's polishing his brass buttons with his fingers. Oh, it's young Jimmy Haighs. Maybe he came by to say hello to his mother."

Caro answered Evie's puzzled look by saying, "Our cook, Mrs. Haighs, has two sons. One is a copper... I mean, a police constable." She turned toward the window. "What are they doing now, Mariah?"

"They are standing by, milady, looking around and now someone else is climbing out of the motor. It's a man in a dark blue suit. He's adjusting his hat and tie and now he's tapping his breast pocket the way some men do as if to check what they think is in the pocket is still there. If you ask me, he wanted to know if he had his little black book." Mariah straightened. "Oh, that can only mean one thing. He's here to ask questions." Mariah turned and looked at Caro as if seeing her in a new light, one filled with suspicion.

"The police are probably going around asking if anyone saw or heard anything," Evie reasoned.

"Mariah, please go let them in. Actually, show him through to the library."

"At once, milady." Mariah ran out of the dining room, her shoes thumping along the floorboards.

When the door closed, Caro whispered, "In the short time I've known her, I've discovered Mariah has rather unique ways about her." After a moment, Caro pushed back her chair and rose to her feet. "I suppose I should go see if I can be of help."

"Would you like us to go with you?" Evie asked.

"Yes, please."

Evie thought she heard her whisper she was still new to this. She supposed Caro meant that, as the lady of the house, she couldn't look to anyone else to make decisions.

Caro led the way to the drawing room. Halfway across the large entry hall, they encountered Mariah rushing toward them.

"It's a detective," Mariah whispered in a worried tone. "And he looks serious."

"Thank you, Mariah." Before entering the library, Caro heaved in a breath and gave a firm nod.

A tall man stood with his back to them. He had one hand inside his pocket and the other holding his hat and he appeared to be studying a painting hanging above the fireplace.

"Good morning, detective."

He turned, his cheeks coloring slightly, almost as if to suggest he had been caught off guard. "Lady Evans. I'm Detective Inspector Marrow."

Caro introduced Evie and Tom. "What's this about, detective?"

"It's actually a courtesy call, my lady. I was hoping to speak with your husband but your maid informed me he is away. While I don't wish to alarm you, I think you should know there has been a death in the village."

A death. Not a murder.

Evie couldn't tell if he was being tactful and considerate in the presence of two ladies or if he had as yet to find any sign of malicious intent.

"We heard about it and we are taking precautions, detective. Is the person a local?"

Evie smiled. They already knew the victim was a woman. Yet, Caro had chosen her words with care.

Not surprisingly, the detective matched Caro's evasion. "We are still trying to identify the... remains. No one has raised the alarm, which suggests the... person might not have been from this village."

Evie glanced at Tom. They had already considered that possibility.

Caro gave an understanding nod. "I suppose you wish to know if we heard or saw anything."

The detective looked down at his hat and ran a finger across the rim. "I assume you haven't. Otherwise, I'm sure you would have contacted the police."

Standing a step behind her, Evie saw Caro still. Would she tell the detective everything they had witnessed the day before?

Caro's shoulders relaxed. "Not necessarily, detective. I might have seen something odd and not really thought much about it at the time. But, hearing your news, it might occur to me that what I saw was indeed and quite possibly of significance."

It seemed Caro had decided to refrain from mentioning their encounter with the bright young things.

The detective's eyebrows drew down. "And… did you?"

Caro somehow managed to avoid a direct response, "I'm sure you'll be speaking with everyone residing in the village. Perhaps you should start at the pub."

"Is there a particular reason why I should do that?" the detective asked.

"There are some people staying there who might be able to assist with your investigation. Then again, it's not my place to say and I'm sure you already had the destination on your list."

He studied Caro for a moment and then nodded and thanked them for their time.

After she showed him out, Caro returned. Pressing her hands to her cheeks, she groaned. "Did I do the right thing? I'm not sure I did. I feel I should have told him everything we know about Lady McAvoy and her entourage, but I felt I didn't want to influence his investigation." Caro paced around the drawing room. "I find myself in an awkward situation. On the one hand, I wish to be of help. Never mind that he didn't actually request it. And, on the other hand, I do have to tread with care. After all, my husband is a detective and I wouldn't want it known I have a keen interest in criminal investigations. This could reflect badly on him..."

Evie gave Caro a moment to work through her doubts and reach her own conclusions.

"Yes, I do believe I was right in not muddling his mind with unnecessary information." Caro looked up. "What do you think?"

Sharing Caro's uncertainty, Evie hesitated, but then she said, "You directed the detective to the pub. He will form his own opinions. And..."

Caro brightened, "And if he doesn't reach the same conclusions we did, we can then enlighten him."

∼

Meanwhile...
Halton House

Millicent hurried her step. She had to share her findings with the dowager and Toodles.

Eliza Barton had been in the library since after breakfast. According to the housemaid, in the time she'd been there adding some water to the flower vase, Eliza had pored over one newspaper after the other.

"What on earth could she be looking for?" Millicent shook her head and focused on what she needed to remember. "Fountain pen. The initials P.L. Alice Barton. Kensington."

She held Holmes against her chest and her attention on the ground because she couldn't afford to ruin another pair of shoes.

When she cleared the gates of the estate, she relaxed but didn't slow down. If anyone saw her leaving the house and asked her about it, she could always say she was running errands for her ladyship. However, everyone was too busy making sure the house would be sparkling by the time her ladyship returned.

She had found a housemaid she could trust to keep an eye on Eliza Barton and keep track of her comings and goings. So, if Eliza left the house, she would know about it.

Finally, Millicent arrived at the dower house, feeling out of breath and in need of a cup of tea. She rang the service entrance door bell and one of the housemaids opened the door.

"You again?" Blocking the entrance, the housemaid crossed her arms.

"Mind what you say to me," Millicent warned.

The housemaid smirked. "That's right. You're her ladyship's maid now. Should I curtsey?"

Disregarding the taunt, Millicent said, "I wish to speak with Lady Henrietta and Toodles." Millicent wished Toodles had remained at Halton House so she wouldn't have to run around so much but, after her ladyship's departure, her ladyship's granny had moved in with the dowager to keep her company.

With a huff, the housemaid stepped back from the door and hitched her head toward the front of the house. "They're in the drawing room. You know the way."

Millicent didn't bother insisting she announce her. She went straight through, knocked on the door and entered the drawing room.

"Ah, Millicent!" the dowager clapped her hands. "We were just talking about you and wondering how you were getting on."

Millicent blurted out, "Fountain pen. The initials P.L. Alice Barton. Kensington."

Looking confused, the dowager looked at Toodles. "I hope she doesn't expect us to guess."

Toodles invited Millicent to sit down before she collapsed.

"Thank you." Millicent didn't dare set Holmes down. She'd already discovered two more cushions thoroughly mangled. As she'd been in a hurry, she'd hidden them... Somewhere.

Eventually, she'd have to hunt around for them and dispose of them properly.

"Now, what's this about a fountain pen, Alice Barton, the initials P.L. and Kensington?" Henrietta raised her hand. "I should ring for some tea first. You look parched."

When the housemaid walked in, Henrietta looked surprised. "Where's Bradley?"

The housemaid blushed. "He's feeling under the weather today, milady."

"This is news to me? Why have I only heard about this now? Never mind... Tell the cook to send up a bowl of her special broth. That should fix Bradley. Now, we would like some tea, please. And some cake. Millicent's stomach is rumbling."

Millicent apologized and explained, "I missed breakfast." Taking a hard swallow, she told them what she had discovered, "Eliza's sister, Alice Barton, works as a housemaid in Kensington. I found a letter... I guess I should start with that. I searched Eliza's bedroom and also found a fountain pen with the initials P.L." Still sounding out of breath, she told them the rest. "What struck me as odd is that her sister assured her she would be on time and would get it right this time. Also, she said she remembered the instructions but she didn't explain what they were."

Sounding excited, Henrietta shifted to the edge of her seat. "Perhaps Eliza entrusted her with a task."

"Do you remember the address in Kensington?" Toodles asked.

Millicent nodded.

"Well, then, we could follow up on that."

Henrietta looked worried. "Are you about to suggest getting in touch with Lotte Mannering? She's already doing enough for us." Smiling, Henrietta turned to Millicent and explained, "I know Evangeline said she would look into it, but I doubt she had the time. So, I contacted the lady detective and asked her to look into the journalists and photographers making their way here. Lotte assured us she would take care of it all."

"Lotte will simply have to find a way to also deal with this," Toodles said. "We'll give her the Kensington address and ask her to follow Alice Barton."

Henrietta's eyes brimmed with excitement. "Oh, this is wonderfully exciting. I'm almost tempted to catch the next train into town."

CHAPTER 17

Primrose Park

After Detective Inspector Marrow left, Caro spent a good half hour trying to decide if she had been right in not telling the detective about Lady McAvoy and her group of rose thieves.

Several times, she decided she had made the right decision, only to then change her mind again. At one point, she grieved for her old life, which she thought had been much simpler, even if, at times, she had played the role of Evie's cousin thrice removed.

Finally, Caro surged to her feet. "I think we've waited long enough. We can't sit here waiting for news and we wouldn't want the detective to think we are trailing after him. But... Yes, most definitely, we must get going now and see what those little bright young beasts are up to."

Stepping out of the house, Caro turned to Mariah. "Lock the door and don't let anyone in."

Mariah's eyes widened. Jumping back, she slammed the front door, turned the key and rushed to the window.

While shocked, Caro gave a nod of approval and made her way to the motor car. "I might have overreacted," she admitted as she settled into her seat. "But you can't be too careful. For all we know, there might be a mad person running around the countryside killing people."

This time, there was no hesitation in setting out. They drove straight to the village and stopped right outside the pub.

During the short drive, they tried to plot out a plan of action. They had already decided they couldn't expect the detective to keep them abreast of the situation.

Caro reasoned, "I suspect he will disapprove of us if he thinks we are in any way involved in an investigation. We should be fine so long as we stay out of his way."

They were surprised to see the quiet village filled with people. At every corner, they saw groups huddled together and talking, no doubt, exchanging what little information they had.

"It seems everyone's found a reason to be outside today," Caro observed.

They saw the police motor car at one end of the street and one of the constables standing outside the post office.

While curious to see what was happening, they remained focused on the pub and its current residents.

"At least we know the bright young things returned," Evie remarked. "They must have arrived in quite a state."

Their roadsters were lined along the street and most of the vehicles were at odd angles.

As they stepped inside the pub, Tom stopped and looked down the street. "The detective just came out of the post office. I suggest we hurry this along. Eventually, he will reach the pub."

Caro raised her chin as if in disdain. "I see the detective is being thorough, starting at one end and working his way from building to building."

"Caro, you're being far too diplomatic." Why would the detective ignore Caro's suggestion he visit the pub? Had he not understood the message? "He really should have listened to you."

"We might all be jumping to conclusions," Tom said. "He might have come here first and only then pursued a more thorough line of investigation."

Inside the pub, they glanced around and found the barkeeper at one end, sweeping the floor and arranging the chairs as he moved along.

Sensing them, he said, "We're not open yet." Looking up, he noticed Caro. "Milady."

Caro stepped forward. "Could we have a word with you, please?"

The barkeeper gave a small nod. "How can I help you, milady?"

"We wanted to know if your guests are still staying at the pub."

"Aye, they came in late last night. Banged on the door well after midnight. I had a good mind to keep them out and let them sleep in the street but they were determined. No sooner did I slide the bolt than they were scrambling inside and making their way up the stairs. A rowdy lot they are and I'll be glad to see the back of 'em."

Evie stepped forward. "What about your other guest? I noticed a woman came in yesterday." She hoped he didn't ask for more details because, other than noticing her entering the pub, Evie hadn't really paid much attention to her.

He looked at the clock behind the bar. "She hasn't come down yet."

"What woman?" Tom whispered.

"I just remembered seeing her yesterday. Right in the midst of the commotion with Lady McAvoy, a woman came in to the pub and she went through a side door." She signaled to the door beside the bar. "I assume it leads upstairs." Evie turned back to the barkeeper. "Has she been staying here long?"

His mouth twisted and he shrugged. "A couple of days."

When he didn't volunteer more information, Evie asked, "Do you know why she's staying here?" If she was visiting family, surely, she would have stayed with them.

"Probably the same reason she always stays here."

"And what might that be?" Caro asked.

"Her sister."

"She has family here?" Evie decided her family might not have a spare room for her.

"Only her sister."

"And where does she live?" Caro asked.

He nudged his head to one side.

Caro's huff suggested she might be growing impatient with the barkeeper. "Do you have an address?"

"The churchyard."

"She works for the vicar?"

"She's resting there."

Caro's voice hitched. "Are you saying she's buried there?"

He gave a shrug followed by a nod.

"Well, why didn't you say so in the first place?" Collecting herself, Caro thanked him and swung around, only to turn back to the barkeeper. "Could you please go knock on your guest's door?"

He gave it some thought and then shook his head. "She might not appreciate being woken up."

Caro stepped forward. "Have you not heard about the woman found dead this morning?"

"Aye, I have. But what's that got to do with Mrs. Read?"

"Mrs. Read?"

"The woman you want me to wake up."

Caro's arms stretched out in frustration and her voice hitched again, "Because she might be the dead woman."

The barkeeper disagreed. "She's most likely still sleeping."

"But we don't know that," Caro insisted.

"I'm not really sure I should do this." Regardless, he set his broom aside and went through the side door.

Tom walked over to the window. "How do we feel about the detective finding us here?"

"Is he coming?" Evie wondered how long it would take the barkeeper to make it up the stairs. They couldn't leave without first finding out if Mrs. Read was still in her room.

"Not yet, but I suspect he is working his way down the

street. He will eventually come to the pub and I'm sure he'll want to know what we're doing here."

Evie frowned. She'd never seen Tom looking and sounding worried. When she pointed this out, he shrugged.

"I'm only thinking of Caro. Remember, she doesn't want to become mixed up in this, whatever this is."

Caro and Evie had their eyes peeled on the door next to the bar. When they heard heavy footsteps approaching, they braced themselves.

"A woman makes a pilgrimage to the village to visit her sister's grave and ends up dead. What are the chances?"

Evie couldn't say.

Caro sighed. "I'll be ecstatically happy if he comes back and says she gave him an earful for waking her up."

The door opened and the barkeeper walked in, his face revealing nothing. Then, his eyes widened as if in disbelief.

When he spoke, his words were devoid of emotion. "Her bed has not been slept in."

"Are you sure?" Caro asked. "Maybe she got up early and made the bed."

"No. My maid has a particular way of making the beds. She used to work in a fancy hotel before she came here to live with her maiden aunt."

Caro turned to Evie. "Can we assume? Dare we assume?"

"Is her luggage still in the room?" Evie asked.

The barkeeper gave a distracted nod.

Evie saw him glance at the broom and imagined him

trying to put the pieces together. One moment he'd been sweeping the floor and the next he'd barged into a guest's room and found she was not there and now… the person might be dead.

They thanked him for his troubles and told him the detective would surely be paying him a visit soon.

When they stepped out of the pub, they all looked down the street and saw one of the constables standing outside a building.

"That's Mrs. Haighs' son, Jimmy. Should we let the detective know what we discovered?" Caro asked.

Evie suggested, "We either tell him or we let him experience the ordeal of questioning the barkeeper."

"Yes, best to tell Jimmy." Caro walked up to the constable and had a quick word with him. When she finished, she returned. "What now?"

Evie drew in a breath. "Now we face the inevitable."

Tom stiffened. "Must we?"

"Mrs. Higgins needs to be told about the fate of her roses."

Relieved, Tom held the motor car door open for them. "Yes, if you must know, I thought you meant we were going to see the dowager."

"Oh, not just yet."

Tom looked heavenward. "With any luck, we will be distracted by some other calamity."

"Actually…" Evie looked down the street. "Before we speak with Mrs. Higgins, I'd like to visit the graveyard."

"It's close enough to walk there," Caro suggested.

Caro and Evie set off toward the church with Tom lagging behind.

As they drew nearer, Evie pointed out the dowager's house.

"Must you do that?" Tom muttered. "You'll only draw attention. Her maid could be looking out the window right now."

Evie leaned in and whispered, "Will the dowager insist on Tom sitting for her?"

"I have no idea. All I know is that she asked, and Tom might have missed his chance to turn her down. Or did she ask? I think she might have just expressed her desire to paint him. Yes, yes, she did."

"What was that?" Tom caught up to them. "I missed it."

"Oh, nothing."

"If there is a way for me to get out of this situation without embarrassing the dowager or myself, please tell me."

"Of course," Caro grinned. "I'll make it my priority to think of something."

The parish church had a well-tended garden and, as they followed a path to the graveyard, they saw more care and attention evident in the manicured lawn and little vases of fresh flowers.

"If Mrs. Read visited the grave recently, we're bound to find flowers," Evie observed. "We'll have to spread out."

Caro leaned down to read a headstone. "Oh, I just realized. We don't know her sister's name."

"I'd suggest looking for a grave with fresh flowers but they all seem to be fairly fresh." Evie tried to think of another way they could identify the grave Mrs. Read had visited.

"This might be the one," Tom pointed to the grave in front of him.

Joining him, Evie looked at the headstone. "Martha Cooper 1871-1896." She did a quick calculation. "She was only twenty-five."

Tom nodded. "The living always have to think of themselves as the exception."

Evie puzzled over his remark. "Because they're living?"

"Precisely. Especially if they make it past the age of twenty-five." He pointed to a grave in the next row. "Despite being in a graveyard, that one ought to consider himself quite the exception. He lived to a ripe old age of ninety-four."

Evie stopped herself from asking why he thought Martha Cooper might be Mrs. Read's sister when she noticed the flowers. "Those look like a Higgins roses."

"Precisely." He glanced around the graveyard. "I don't see any other Higgins roses."

Evie gasped and pressed her hand to her chest.

"Countess? Did you see something?"

"Oh, how odd. That's exactly what you asked me at the garden party. I just remembered something. I had noticed a woman standing on the edge of the garden. One moment she was there, and the next she was gone. At first, I thought it might have been one of the gardeners. Then, I thought it might have been someone local who'd come to have a look at the guests. What if it was Mrs. Read?"

CHAPTER 18

*E*vie looked toward the church. "There is only one way that I can think of to confirm if this grave belongs to Mrs. Read's sister. Or, at least, find some information to connect Mrs. Reid to this grave. The parish registers. We'll have to do some digging around to make the connection. With any luck, Martha Cooper's parents married and baptized their children here."

"I'll go have a word with the vicar," Caro offered.

As they waited, Tom and Evie strolled around the graveyard.

"I don't see any other Higgins roses. That must be the grave. While this might be a stab in the dark, I'm assuming the presence of the Higgins rose connects Mrs. Read to the woman I saw standing at the edge of Mrs. Higgins' garden." Evie stopped at another grave to read the headstone and then turned away. Definitely far too young, she thought.

Caro emerged from the church shaking her head. Reaching them, she said, "The vicar is visiting a parishioner and won't be back until later today. His housekeeper was arranging the flowers and she didn't think it right for us to look at the registers without the vicar present."

"Perhaps we can come back," Evie suggested. "Meanwhile..." her shoulders dropped. "I am not looking forward to this but we must call on Mrs. Higgins. It's not just that I'm afraid she will not take the news well, I'm also concerned about not having any worthwhile information for her. Just as well I'm not charging for my services. I'd have to refund the fees."

"Don't let Lotte hear you say that," Tom laughed. "I'm sure there is an acceptable margin of error or level of failure."

"Not in my books. Mrs. Higgins is emotionally invested in me finding a favorable outcome."

Caro dug around her small handbag. "I should start carrying around some writing implements and paper. How am I supposed to remember everything we have to tell the detective?"

"Does that mean you have decided to share our information with him?" Evie asked.

"No, I've just changed my mind again. I'm not sure he's the type to appreciate an outsider's input and I wouldn't want him to spread gossip about me." Caro shuddered. "I can just picture Henry becoming cross and punching him."

"That's quite an imagination you have, Caro. Why would Henry do that?"

"The detective might label me some sort of upstart busybody. Henry knows I'm highly sensitive about my background. When he returns, I suppose I should have a word with him and tell him I will be perfectly fine and I can stand up for myself." She hesitated for a moment and then gave a decisive nod. "Yes, indeed. I wouldn't want Henry to clash with a colleague over me."

Walking back toward the pub, they saw one of the constables standing outside, his hands behind his back as he glanced one way and then the other.

"Finally," Caro exclaimed. "The detective has found his way to the pub. Should we wait and see if he wishes to talk with us?" Drawing in a breath, Caro answered her own question. "No, I really think we should steer clear of his investigation."

That left them with no option but to pay Mrs. Higgins a visit. During the short drive, Evie wondered if she should bring up the subject of Mrs. Read. Would telling Mrs. Higgins someone else had also taken her roses open fresh wounds?

She turned to Caro. "I've just realized we don't have confirmation about the identity of the body."

"No, we don't, but I really didn't want to wait for the detective. I've been worrying about how he will perceive our involvement and, despite telling Constable Haighs about Mrs. Reid, I insist the only solution is to avoid the detective." Looking stony-faced, Caro added, "If you hear me change my mind again, please stop me. In fact, feel free to elbow me in the ribs."

"Caro, you're developing worry lines," Evie warned.

When they reached the Higgins' house, a butler showed them through to a drawing room with an uninterrupted vista of the gardens. They could see a couple of gardeners tending to the rose bushes with Mrs. Higgins overseeing the process of pruning the ruined roses.

"I'm glad to see her out and about." Evie hoped she would put the malicious act behind her and focus on encouraging new blooms.

They watched the butler making his way out to the gardens. When he reached Mrs. Higgins, he stopped at a discreet distance and waited for her to notice him. When she did, she looked surprised. Evie thought she must have been lost in her passionate pursuit not to have heard the motor car driving up to the house.

The butler received his instructions and turned toward the house. Before he'd even made it halfway across the lawn, the daughter of the house, Annabelle, entered the drawing room.

Seeing them, her brilliant smile wavered for a moment.

Had she been expecting someone else?

Annabelle recovered and greeted them.

"How is your mother faring?" Evie asked.

"As you can see, she's thrown herself into the task of restoring her garden." She glanced out the window and then asked, "Do you have news?"

As Evie tried to work out how best to describe the fate of the roses, Mrs. Higgins walked in, showing no trace of the previous day's distress.

"How lovely to see you all again."

The fact she looked so jovial made Evie's task that much harder. She couldn't think of a time when she'd dreaded being the bearer of bad news as much as she did that moment. She relayed the information as succinctly as possible and watched Mrs. Higgins' happiness shatter.

"But why?" she exclaimed. "Why would they do that?"

"We think they were driven by their desire to enhance their performance," Evie explained. "It's… it's what they do. I believe it has something to do with the element of shock."

"Are they regular guests?" Caro asked.

"Heavens, no." Mrs. Higgins looked at her daughter. "In fact, we were puzzled by their presence."

Caro looked intrigued by the news and sought confirmation. "So, you didn't invite them?"

"Absolutely not. I still assume they came as someone else's guests."

"Do you have any idea who might have invited them?"

Mrs. Higgins studied her daughter. The young woman's cheeks colored and while she tried her best to hold her mother's gaze, she ended up averting her eyes.

"Annabelle. You told me you didn't know."

"I don't, Mamma."

"But you have your suspicions?"

If Evie had to guess, she'd say they were referring to Frederick. But why would he invite the group to a garden party?

Heavens. Had he meant to play some sort of mischievous trick on Mrs. Higgins?

"I should apologize. This is not the time to have a family discussion." Mrs. Higgins turned to her daughter again. "Ring for some tea, please."

"That would be lovely, Mrs. Higgins, but I'm afraid we must be going." Evie made a move to get up. While she didn't wish to delay their departure, curiosity got the better of her. "Actually, I meant to ask you if you knew Mrs. Read."

Mrs. Higgins' cheeks paled. "The name sounds familiar. But I'm not sure where I've heard it mentioned."

"Mamma? Isn't she the lady who visits you every so often?"

"Annabelle, I feel a draft. Could you please do something about it?" Mrs. Higgins waited for her daughter to leave the room before saying, "I'm sorry, what were you saying?"

Caro jumped in, saying, "We wondered if you knew Mrs. Read. I'm sure you've heard about the incident in the village."

Mrs. Higgins' fingers wrapped around the armrest. "Incident?"

"Yes, a woman has been found dead."

"Oh, dear." Mrs. Higgins looked over her shoulder. "Where is that girl with the tea? Did Annabelle even ring for it? I'm sure she didn't." Mrs. Higgins sprung to her feet and reached for the cord next to the fireplace. "Did you say dead?"

Caro nodded. "Yes. The police are investigating the matter. In fact, they are going around the village talking with everyone. They're bound to eventually come here."

"But why would they wish to speak with me?"

Evie explained, "Because they are investigating the death. You might be able to assist in their investigation. Perhaps you saw something or heard something…" Leaning forward, Evie studied Mrs. Higgins' face as she asked, "How did you know Mrs. Read?"

Mrs. Higgins looked away as if distracted. "I... I wouldn't exactly say I knew her. Why would you even ask me about her?"

"We know she visited the village on a regular basis." Evie considered mentioning the fact she might have seen her at the garden party. "We saw some flowers in a grave. It was a pretty bouquet with some Higgins roses."

Mrs. Higgins pressed her hand to her chest. "My roses?"

Evie suspected Mrs. Higgins was about to do her best to distract them by pretending she didn't know anything about Mrs. Read or the roses.

Before the next thought could take shape in Evie's mind, Mrs. Higgins' expression changed from shocked to insouciant. "The gardeners are sometimes approached by people. They might have given her the roses. Yes, it's quite possible that's what happened. Or... Sometimes, people wander into the garden and help themselves."

Evie persevered. "A moment ago, your daughter suggested Mrs. Read visited you."

Mrs. Higgins' shoulder lifted slightly. "Annabelle mistook her for someone else."

Evie found herself wondering what Lotte Mannering would do in this situation. One moment Mrs. Higgins admitted to being familiar with the name only to then deny knowing Mrs. Read.

To their surprise, Mrs. Higgins rose to her feet. "I must apologize. I just remembered I have an appointment." She walked to the door, bringing their discussion to an abrupt end.

Outside, as they walked toward the motor car, Caro looked dumbfounded. "What just happened?"

"We were shown the door." Evie didn't want to add to Caro's worry lines by saying they would definitely need to have a word with the detective. As a trained professional, he would know how to extract the information from Mrs. Higgins.

Once they were on their way, Caro laughed.

Evie waited a moment to see if she would share the joke. When she didn't, she had to ask, "What's so amusing?"

Caro tried to change the subject. "Mrs. Higgins is hiding something."

"Yes, I agree. But why were you laughing?"

Caro smiled at her. "Only someone who's worked in service would understand it."

Evie ran through the conversation they'd had with Mrs. Higgins but she couldn't detect anything that might have caused such amusement. "Caro, if you don't tell me, I'll toss and turn all night."

Caro relented. "I feel a draft?"

Evie smiled but Caro had been right, she didn't understand the joke.

Sensing her puzzlement, Caro felt compelled to explain, "In one of my previous places of employment, the lady of the house would ring the bell. John, a new footman, always complained because he'd walk up the three floors, and when he entered the room, the lady of the house would say, "John, I feel a draft. Do something about it." She'd then give the fireplace a pointed look. John couldn't understand why she couldn't simply say to add a log or poke the fire. Or even get up and do it herself instead of ringing for a servant. Then another footman explained that if she said exactly what she wanted, he would think that she knew how fires worked and that would lower her to his level and defeat the purpose of having servants."

"Good heavens, did I ever do that to you?"

Caro gave it some thought. "Not that I recall. Then again, Tom is always hovering by the fireplace. Anyhow, what do you think? Is Mrs. Higgins hiding something?"

"Absolutely. She knew Mrs. Read but she pretended she didn't. Or, rather, she played down her acquaintance and, then, she completely denied it." Evie leaned forward to speak to Tom. "I hope you remember we are going to see the dowager."

Tom's shoulders sagged. Tapping his fingers on the steering wheel, he squared his shoulders and tipped his hat down.

"Actually, Tom. You should stop for a moment. We need to talk about this. I wonder if Mrs. Higgins realizes she has now stoked our curiosity. Why she denied knowing Mrs. Reid is now a burning question."

Tom slowed down and brought the motor car to a stop.

"She could be hiding something petty or of such significance, it could make her world unravel." Caro smiled. "I know that sounds rather dramatic, but we should consider all possibilities."

Evie agreed. "Her daughter said Mrs. Reid visited often and Mrs. Higgins was quick to refute it. Do we believe the mother or the daughter?"

"I agree with Caro. Without solid proof," Tom said, "we should keep our minds open to any and all possibility."

"All possibilities? That means more work for us since we'll have to invest as much time on each idea." And, Evie thought, that went against the process of an investigation since, usually, one had to decide which avenues to pursue and which to abandon. "Should we then work on the assumption Mrs. Higgins lied? If so, we must assume the connection to Mrs. Reid is of significance."

Caro gave a firm nod. "She must have something to lose or a secret she doesn't want revealed."

Evie and Caro saw the detective emerging from a store at the end of the street.

"We might need to find a way to engage with the detective." Seeing Caro's worry lines deepening, Evie added, "Although… I think we should find a way to encourage him to seek our assistance."

CHAPTER 19

"You'd think the murder of a few roses at the garden party would be the worst of criminal activities in the district," Caro complained.

While Evie didn't want to think about murderous intentions lurking around every corner, she assumed the criminal mind knew no limits or boundaries. "There is a reason why the police are kept so busy. However, I understand your thinking. Until a couple of years ago I hadn't thought about crime. In fact, I'd been thoroughly oblivious to it."

Tom drove along the main street of the village at a sedate pace. Leaning back, he said, "Don't you think it's dreadfully inconsiderate of us to drop in on Louisa without prior notice or an invitation?"

Sounding worried, Evie said, "You're right. She could be in the middle of an inspired painting session."

Caro groaned and slid down in her seat. "One of these days it will happen and I fear I won't be prepared and I'll probably run out of the house shrieking."

Tom straightened. "Brace yourselves. There's a motor car outside the house."

Caro shot up and leaned forward. "Oh, I recognize it. I'm sure it belongs to Lord Melville."

"The motor car does look familiar. Is he known for visiting Louisa?" Evie asked.

Caro gave it some thought. "I've never heard her mention a visit from him. Then again, I really haven't known Mamma that long. While she described him to us, that doesn't necessarily mean she knows him socially."

"Perfect," Evie declared. "That can only mean he has a very particular reason for visiting her now. Yes, yes, I know, I'm jumping to conclusions. However, today is rather a different day. A woman has been found dead. We should be on the lookout for anyone acting out of character."

As Tom brought the motor car to a stop behind the fancy Rolls Royce, Evie glanced back toward the village. The manor house provided an uninterrupted view of the main street. If Louisa chose to, she could watch everyone's comings and goings. And, if not Louisa, then her gossipy maid.

Descending from the motor car, Evie looked at the chauffeur. After a moment of studying his features, she remembered seeing him at the garden party. Despite smiling at him, his hard features did not soften. Indeed, he barely acknowledged them as they walked by.

"I think Lord Melville's snobbishness has rubbed off on his chauffeur," Evie whispered.

They rang the doorbell and were welcomed by one of the housemaids.

"That's Lily, the gossipy housemaid," Caro whispered when they were shown through to the drawing room.

The moment Louisa saw them enter, her eyes lit up. "Oh, fabulous. I hope you have brought news."

Lord Melville jumped to his feet. He wore a light beige suit with a pale green tie and appeared to be surprised by their visit. He fidgeted with his pocket and finally stood with his hands clasped behind his back, his eyes jumping from one piece of furniture to the other.

The dowager introduced Lord Melville, adding, "Melville has called on me in the hope that I would have fresh news about today's events."

He took a step back until he reached the fireplace. With his head tilted up as though they had brought a bad smell with them, he said, "Yes, nasty business this and no one seems to know anything."

"There's a detective on the case," Evie offered. "Detective Inspector Morrow. I believe he is keen to speak with everyone."

Lord Melville seemed to be taken aback by the news. "Well, he hasn't spoken with me."

"I'm sure he will eventually get to you, Melville. What will you say?" Louisa asked, her eyes twinkling with amusement.

"That I know nothing, of course." His lip curled as if he'd suddenly caught a whiff of something distasteful. "Do we even know who it is?"

The dowager gave Caro a pointed look. "Caro? I'm sure you have discovered something by now."

"Nothing of importance, Mamma."

Lord Melville appeared to grow even taller. "Well, I

suppose I should make myself available at home." He turned to Louisa. "It's been lovely to see you again."

To Evie's surprise and amusement, he expressed delight over making their acquaintance. Yet, during the brief encounter, he hadn't once looked at any of them. Remembering the dowager saying he was a snob, Evie could only assume Lord Melville did not care for the new Lady Evans, the American born Countess of Woodridge or plain Tom Winchester.

The moment he stepped out of the drawing room, the air itself seemed to lighten. If Louisa found him disagreeable, she did not say.

"Louisa, I hope I'm not being too intrusive by asking if Lord Melville is a close acquaintance," Evie said.

Louisa laughed. "Good heavens, no, he isn't. The only reason Lily showed him through is because she's cranky with me. Otherwise, I would not have been at home."

"Cranky?"

"Yes, it appears I threw a shoe at her last night. As usual, she remembered something or other and couldn't wait until morning to tell me. Honestly, if I had thrown a shoe at her, I think I would have remembered. In any case, I hope she has now calmed down. I couldn't really take another visit from the local gentry wishing to use my view of the village for their own purposes. The entire time he was here he stood by the window looking out. I finally lost interest in looking at the back of his head and ordered him to sit down." Louisa's smile spoke of pleasure and mischief. "I might have snapped at him and startled him. He reacted so abruptly, he nearly hit the ceiling."

Caro looked at Evie. "Just as you thought. He came here to spy on the village. Or, rather, to spy on the detective."

Yes, but what did that mean? Did he fear discovery? Only someone with something to hide would show any real concern.

"Mamma, I hope you won't mind feeding us," Caro said in a casual tone.

"Of course not. It will give the cook something to do." She rang the bell and gave the maid instructions. Waiting for the door to close, Louisa leaned in and murmured, "So, have you brought news?"

Caro took care of relating their morning's adventures.

"You visited the graveyard?" Louisa sat back. "That's interesting. My maid went out this morning and returned with a story about Lord Melville being seen having words with a woman in the graveyard." Louisa looked up. "Oh, wait a minute. I think she conveyed that tidbit a couple of nights ago. In any case, since she didn't have a specific description of the woman, it could be any number of people. However," she held up a finger, "that reminds me of something. As I said, my maid has the habit of waking me up in the middle of the night to impart some news or other she forgot to tell me during the day. Anyhow, a few days ago, that's precisely what she did, saying it was that time of the year again and Cooper has flowers."

"Cooper!" Excited by the news, Caro declared, "That's the grave Evie and Tom identified because of the Higgins roses. We think the person who visited the grave is Mrs. Reid. She's staying at the pub, only… her bed hasn't been slept in. Which reminds me, we should have stopped at the pub to ask if she has made an appearance."

"Have you shared this information with the detective?" Louisa asked.

"No. We don't wish to impose. Although, I did pass on the information to the young constable."

The dowager signaled to the window. "You might have to speak with the detective yourself. In fact, there he is."

Caro stiffened. "Where?"

"He's just walking up to the house. That's interesting. He actually took a moment to glance at my roses." Louisa hummed under her breath. "I believe that's a good sign. It shows he is observant. Or maybe he's had a difficult morning and wishes to rest his mind and eyes."

Evie turned to look at Tom and had to search for him. He'd chosen a chair in a corner, well away from Louisa's line of vision and looked positively distraught to have been discovered.

Caro jumped to her feet and paced around the drawing room.

"My goodness." The dowager smiled at Caro. "What on earth is the matter with you?"

Caro stopped and swung around to face them. "When the detective comes in, we shouldn't speak unless spoken to."

The door opened and the maid announced the detective.

He walked in and looked surprised to see them but recovered quickly. "I was hoping to have a word with Lady Evans."

"Oh? Which one?" Louisa asked.

"My apologies, I meant to say the Dowager Lady Evans."

Looking pleased and relieved, Caro stepped back.

"Detective, I will spare you the trouble. I saw nothing and I heard nothing." Louisa lifted her chin. "Have you identified the body?"

He nodded. "The barkeeper confirmed it for us a short while ago. The victim is Mrs. Reid."

Evie waited for him to say he had followed Caro's lead. To her annoyance, he made no mention of it.

"Well, then." The dowager's eyes twinkled. "Everyone here can offer their assistance because they knew that before you discovered it."

Evie turned to look at Louisa and saw the edges of her eyes crinkling with amusement. It seemed Lady Louisa Evans rather enjoyed stoking the fire.

The maid walked in. Before she could speak, Louisa said, "Lily, please tell the cook there will be another guest staying for luncheon."

The maid hesitated, her eyes darting to the detective. After a moment, she said, "Certainly, milady," and stepped out of the drawing room.

The detective looked out of his depth. In fact, he and Caro had both stopped blinking.

After spending an entire morning changing her mind about whether or not she would share information with the detective, Caro now looked cornered.

"Mamma, I'm sure the detective has many people he wishes to speak with and needs to get on with his job but he's too polite to say anything."

"Nonsense. He has to eat. There's no point in carrying

out an investigation on an empty stomach. Besides, he needs to hear about the connections you made. He might learn a thing or two."

"Connections?" the detective asked and looked straight at Caro.

As her lady's maid, Caro had never shown any hesitation in sharing her opinions. However, as Lady Evans, she appeared to think twice before speaking, which showed a great deal of caution.

"Does it have something to do with the reason you directed me to the pub earlier today, my lady?" he asked.

Out of the corner of her eye, Evie saw Tom shift in his seat and cross his legs as if making himself comfortable to watch a performance.

When Caro appeared to flounder, Louisa spoke up. "Caro is probably too modest to stake a claim, detective. The fact of the matter is that she and her friends knew the identity of the dead body before you did. Heavens, did I just repeat myself?" Louisa turned to Caro. "If you hear me repeating myself, please feel free to tell me so, Caro. I don't wish to acquire the trait before my time."

The detective frowned. "You knew the identity? Lady Evans, this morning when I spoke with you, you said you hadn't seen or heard anything."

"Strictly speaking, we didn't." Caro cleared her throat and glanced at Evie.

"Detective," Evie said, "Lady Louisa gives us too much credit. We were simply in the right place at the right time and happened to notice some details and then we were fortunate enough to add them all together. However, at the time, we weren't really sure what we had seen or what it all meant. And, without any accurate information at our disposal, we were only guessing."

The detective held her gaze for a moment. "You mentioned noticing details. Details you did not share with me."

"Only because we didn't wish to impede or in any way misdirect your investigation," Evie explained.

The detective reached inside his pocket and drew out his little black notebook and pen. Uncapping his pen, he gave a nod. "Any time you're ready, Lady Woodridge," he turned to Caro, "Lady Evans. I should like to hear the whole story."

"Detective, this is merely about chance encounters. We happened to be at the pub when I noticed Mrs. Reid entering. At the time, of course, I didn't make the connection. Indeed, I only saw a woman and noticed her the way you might notice anyone walking into a room. But, later, I remembered thinking I had seen her at a garden party we attended earlier in the day."

"Which day might this be."

"Yesterday. And, I'm still not entirely sure it was the same person. Anyhow, then, we discovered Mrs. Reid came to the village once a year to visit her sister's grave. At that point, we only knew she hadn't slept in her bed, but it was enough to trigger our suspicions."

"How exactly did you ascertain that information?" he asked.

If she answered truthfully, Evie knew she would expose them to the fact they had been looking into the death with more than just a passing interest. Unfortunately, she saw no way around it. "We asked the barkeeper to check her room."

"What prompted you to ask?"

Evie glanced at Tom. Seeing him raising an eyebrow, she imagined him saying, *Yes, Countess, what prompted you to ask?*

Evie drew in a long breath. "We thought that if someone from the village had gone missing, the alarm would have been raised. When we discovered Mrs. Reid did not live in the village, we were keen to establish her whereabouts. As the barkeeper had mentioned she came to the village every year to visit her sister's grave, we searched for it and made the connection to the garden party." She stopped for a moment and realized she hadn't actually answered his question.

"How exactly did you make a connection?"

Evie searched her mind and retraced their steps. "The Higgins rose."

By this point, the detective looked thoroughly confused.

"Why exactly have you been interested in Mrs. Reid?"

"That part doesn't really matter."

"With all due respect, my lady, I would like to be the judge of that."

Abandoning her earlier hesitation, Caro spoke up, "We were investigating the theft of some roses. Higgins roses, to be precise. At that point, we were not interested in Mrs. Reid. Although, as it turned out, she helped herself to some roses. Or, perhaps, one of the gardeners gave them to her. We can't be sure because Mrs. Higgins wouldn't say."

"Mrs. Higgins?"

Caro gave a firm nod. "Yes, she hosted the garden party we attended."

"May I ask why you were investigating the theft of roses?"

Caro chirped, "There's a simple explanation for that. Mrs. Higgins engaged Lady Woodridge's services."

He looked at Evie. "Why would Mrs. Higgins do that?"

"Because Lady Woodridge is a Lady Detective and her reputation preceded her."

The detective sat back and studied Evie.

"Detective, you could ask my husband about Lady Woodridge's credentials. In the past, she has been quite helpful. Indeed, she has been instrumental in the capture of several criminals."

"You've assisted Detective Inspector Evans?"

He didn't sound convinced and Evie didn't blame him. Everything they'd told him they'd seen had been disjointed, haphazard and nothing short of coincidental. "Our paths have crossed once or twice."

The detective tapped his notebook. "Tell me more about Mrs. Higgins."

Evie could not have been more surprised by his question as she'd expected the detective to issue a warning about meddling in police business.

When she finished telling him all they knew, including their recent visit to Mrs. Higgins, she added, "It seems odd that she would change her mind about knowing Mrs. Reid."

The housemaid walked in and announced, "Luncheon is ready."

The detective surged to his feet, thanked Louisa for the kind invitation, which he declined, and offered a hasty apology for leaving before Louisa could even think of insisting he stay for lunch.

"I must say, I'm surprised he didn't choose to stay for luncheon. I know I have at least a dozen questions to ask." Louisa led them through to the dining room. "Let's put our heads together. I'd like to see if we can find the culprit before he does."

Evie thought she heard Tom agree with the idea. Knowing him, she assumed he would like nothing better than to keep Louisa engaged in something other than painting.

∽

Meanwhile...
The kitchen, Halton House

Millicent stabbed a pea. She'd been trying to enjoy her lunch while working on her plan to expose Eliza Barton for the person she... might be... but could barely focus with the constant chatter drowning out her thoughts.

"There's a fair coming to the village next week," Joseph, one of the footmen, declared, shooting Eliza a bright smile.

"That sounds like a lot of fun. We should all go together," Eliza suggested.

Millicent snorted. Eliza Barton had made herself quite comfortable in her new position and now everyone was her friend.

The back-door doorbell rang.

"I'll go see who it is," Joseph offered.

When he returned, he held up an envelope. "It's for Millicent."

"And why do you have to sound so surprised," Millicent chided.

"Because you only get mail once a month and it arrived last week." He turned the envelope. "It must be something very important if the dowager sent her chauffeur to deliver the message."

The dowager had written to her?

Millicent's chin lifted. "Not at all. Otherwise, the dowager would have come herself."

"You've become very cheeky since taking over from Caro," Joseph teased.

"It's Lady Evans, if you don't mind. She earned it." Millicent took the envelope, drew out the piece of paper and read it. "Now, if you'll excuse me, I must compose a reply." Millicent strolled out of the kitchen. When she reached the stairs, she rushed up.

"Lotte is chasing up those special books you wanted," she read. What on earth did the dowager mean? She didn't remember talking about books. Had the dowager confused her with someone else?

Millicent read the note again. It didn't make sense. The lady detective was already looking into the journalists and photographers and following Eliza Barton's sister. Why would the dowager burden the lady detective with another task?

"Oh!" Millicent drew in a sharp breath. The dowager had sent her a secret message in code.

They already had enough mysteries to contend with.

Why add another one?

CHAPTER 20

*L*uncheon with the dowager had given them an opportunity to sit back and let someone else do most of the talking and thinking.

"Mamma has a sharp mind," Caro remarked.

"Yes, I'd almost forgotten about Lady McAvoy. I'm glad Louisa brought up the subject." So far, the wayward group hadn't caused any more havoc in the village. Yet, they remained here.

Tom murmured, "I'm just glad Louisa focused on Lady McAvoy and Mrs. Reid's death instead of harping on about wanting to paint me. While she hasn't mentioned it again, the way she looks at me..." he grumbled under his breath. "Forget I said any of that."

They sat in the motor car looking down the village street and could see the roadsters still parked outside the pub.

"What do you think they're still doing here?" Caro asked.

Evie fished around her mind for possible reasons.

"They might still be sleeping. Some people take the idea of keeping gentlemen hours quite seriously. Or, perhaps the detective asked them to remain for a while longer. It's even possible they made the decision to remain. They might be interested to see if the detective catches the murderer—" Evie stopped and stared ahead.

"Countess?"

She looked at Tom, her thoughts fixated on that last remark. "I've only just realized we don't even know how Mrs. Reid died. The detective didn't volunteer the information and we didn't ask."

"You're right," Caro exclaimed. "I don't recall the detective mentioning it."

"Should we hunt him down?" Tom asked. "He owes us the information. It would be a fair exchange after all the observations you shared with him."

Evie chortled. "I'm not sure any of it was of any use."

Tom looked over his shoulder. "I'm feeling uneasy about just sitting here. The motor is running and I'm ready to take us somewhere."

"I suggest we return to the house and work on a strategy. Tom's right, Mamma is likely wondering what we're still doing here. She might send Lily out to ask Tom to step inside for a sitting."

Evie and Caro were suddenly pushed back as the motor car took off.

After a moment, Caro turned to Evie. "I feel I should apologize. You came here for a relaxing visit and now we're in the middle of a murder investigation."

"It's not your fault, Caro. Besides, I'm the one who insisted we should go to the garden party. If we hadn't attended, we might not have been drawn into any of this."

"It's strange to find myself dealing with a murder in our village," Caro mused. "When you suggested Henry and I marry at the local parish church instead of here, I must admit I entertained a few reservations. In fact, the night before the wedding, I tossed and turned thinking someone would be murdered and we'd have to postpone the wedding."

Evie had no idea how to respond to the revelation. She thought she heard Tom murmur, "The Countess of Doom."

He must have because Caro stifled a giggle.

Crossing her arms, Evie sat back. "I hope you're not suggesting trouble follows me wherever I go."

Instead of denying it, Caro tilted her head. "That hadn't occurred to me. Do you think it's possible for someone to have that effect on their surroundings? Are any of us safe in your company?"

Evie lifted her chin and looked away. "I'm sure there have been other crimes committed elsewhere. In fact, I assume your husband is currently investigating one."

"I shouldn't tease you. If not for your observations, quite a few crimes might still remain unsolved."

When they arrived at Primrose Park, Evie made the firm decision to put the events of the previous day behind her. She had played her part and had shared all she'd seen with the detective. Now, she would enjoy Caro's company and the remainder of their visit.

They climbed out of the motor car and walked up to the front door. To their surprise, no one opened the door.

Evie had never experienced that before. Normally, when she arrived somewhere there was a footman or even a butler waiting for her…

Caro gave Evie a nervous glance and rang the doorbell.

When the front door remained closed, Caro rang the doorbell again. "I'm sure someone will be along soon."

After a few more minutes, they heard footsteps running across the hall and expected the door to finally open. When it didn't, they all leaned in.

Just then, the door opened a fraction and Mariah peered out. "Is that you, milady?"

"Yes, Mariah. We would like to come inside now, please."

"I just looked out the window and saw the motor car but I couldn't see you." Mariah gave a stiff nod. "You should be quick about it, milady. We don't know who could be lurking out there. We were all beginning to worry."

"You should stop worrying, Mariah," Caro assured her. "The detective is on the case and will, no doubt, bring the perpetrator to justice in no time."

Mariah jumped back. "So, he hasn't caught him yet? Mrs. Haighs won't like the sound of that. She's been saying she's quite happy to sleep under the stairs, in the kitchen or in the pantry."

"If Mrs. Haighs wishes to stay here the night, then she can have a proper room. Could we have some tea brought into the library, please?"

Mariah nodded and swung away only to turn back and rush to the front door. "I'll bolt it, just in case."

"Have Steven and Peter returned?" Caro asked, but Mariah had already disappeared down the hall. "I guess I'll play footman." Caro took Evie and Tom's hats and removed her own hat.

They walked into the library and settled down to enjoy a moment of silence broken only when Tom remarked, "You have quite a collection of books."

"Most of them came with the house but Henry has his own collection which is mostly in his study," Caro said and pointed to a set of double doors. "Henry likes to keep abreast of scientific and criminology discoveries so he does a great deal of reading." She walked to a small table by the fireplace and picked up a book. "He's been reading to me from this book. *Criminology*. At first, I thought it would put me to sleep but I actually find it fascinating."

Studying the books on the shelves, Tom said, "It looks like his relatives were also interested in criminology." He smiled and, with a hint of surprise in his voice, added, "And fairy tales."

"Fairy tales?"

Tom pointed to a collection of books.

"I hadn't noticed those. Then again, I haven't had much time to explore the house."

As Tom and Caro discussed the contents of the library, Evie found herself thinking about Mrs. Reid. She had been found on the road. Without specific details, she could only wonder if she had been found on the road, by the side of the road or in a ditch.

Mostly, she wanted to know what took place just before Mrs. Reid died.

Evie considered the possibility Mrs. Reid had been on

her way somewhere, perhaps to meet someone. While the weather had been pleasant, Evie doubted Mrs. Reid had trekked out for a stroll in the middle of the night. That opened quite a few avenues of inquiries. Why had she gone out so late at night? To keep the meeting secret, Evie thought.

She'd either been headed to someone's house or had planned on meeting someone in a quiet part of the road, away from the village.

Evie sat back and drummed her fingers on the armrest.

She pictured the person Mrs. Reid had been waiting for approaching, either by foot or in a vehicle.

Closing her eyes, she tried to draw a clearer picture of the scene.

In her mind, she saw Mrs. Reid swinging around as she heard the crunch of footsteps on the road.

Dissatisfied with that image, Evie amended the story. Mrs. Reid heard a motor car approaching and braced herself for the encounter.

The mystery person and Mrs. Reid talked in hurried whispers.

Evie leaned forward.

She pictured the conversation between Mrs. Reid and the person she'd set out to meet becoming intense. Then, they argued. One of them became aggressive. Finally, one of them lost their temper and…

"Countess?"

Evie looked up, only then realizing she'd dug her fingers into the armrest.

"You look horror stricken," Tom said.

Evie's thoughts scattered. "Oh… I've… I've been trying to picture Mrs. Reid by the side of the road."

"That's a gruesome image to entertain."

Evie shrugged. "It's difficult to imagine what happened. Do you think she knew her assailant? Even if we had access to that information, how would we find the motive? There has to be a motive."

Caro returned the book she'd been perusing to the shelf and went to sit next to Evie. "If she knew her assailant, it could be someone from the village." Caro gasped. "I know we've been assuming that all along, but it's only now registered in my mind. There could be a murderer living among us."

"Here's another thought. Or, rather, a question," Evie said. "Did the assailant go to meet her willingly or did Mrs. Reid use coercion to draw them out? Meet me or else." Evie thought that would fit in with the theory she had been considering.

"In case you've forgotten, Countess, Louisa's maid said Lord Melville had been seen having words with a woman in the graveyard."

Could they really suspect Lord Melville of being the mystery person who'd met Mrs. Reid?

Would he argue with someone in public?

"I'm sure Lord Melville has a solid alibi for the night in question." Caro smiled. "Just listen to me. I'm sounding like Henry."

Evie tossed the thought around in her mind. "Even if he has an alibi, Lord Melville made a point of visiting Louisa. That could be a sign of concern. Of course, he could just be worried that someone saw him arguing with

Mrs. Reid. It's the sort of information one can easily misconstrue. I'm already jumping to conclusions and thinking he might have had a reason to harm Mrs. Reid. Heavens, we need more reliable information. We don't even know if she's the woman he was seen arguing with."

Evie tried to capture her earlier train of thought. Where had it been leading her? "If Mrs. Reid didn't set out to meet someone, then we have to assume she was headed somewhere. It couldn't have been too far from the village."

The fact she had set off on a walk in the middle of the night suggested she'd had an ulterior motive.

"We know Lord Melville's estate is quite close," Caro offered. "It's certainly within walking distance of the village. But it would have been too dark."

"I wonder what Lord Melville and Mrs. Reid argued about. That is, assuming Mrs. Reid was the person he argued with. The lack of factual information is not helping." And Evie couldn't think of a way around that without making their meddling obvious to the detective.

They all stared into space and were so involved in their thoughts they barely noticed the sound of hurried steps approaching the library.

The door opened and Mariah walked in. "Milady, it's Peter and Steven. They have returned from the village. Shall I tell them to come in? I was too excited to see them and didn't ask if they had news. But I'm sure they do."

The footmen didn't wait to be summoned. They stepped up to the door and peered in.

Caro beckoned them inside. "Have you been in the village all this time? We didn't see you."

"We were mingling, milady, hoping to eavesdrop on

people's conversations but no one knew anything. So, we decided to come back. Along the way, Steven had a puncture and we had to stop to fix it. Then, we had to answer the call of nature so we walked off the road and found a copse of trees."

The footman, Steven, elbowed Peter in the ribs.

"I mean…"

"Yes, I know what you mean, Peter. Go on. What happened next?" Caro encouraged.

"That's when we heard the roadsters driving by. Steven was worried they would pinch the bicycles as a lark so we hurried back to the road and saw them stop a short distance away."

Steven nodded and shifted, looking either uncomfortable or uncertain. At a signal from Peter, he picked up the story. "Another motor car approached them. We had no trouble recognizing it because it's the only Rolls Royce around like it."

Lord Melville's motor car? Evie wondered if that was the connection they'd been looking for. They knew the night before Lady McAvoy and her friends had driven toward his house, but they had no way of confirming it, not even after hearing this latest information.

Steven continued, "We were too far to hear the conversation but they spoke for about ten minutes and then the Rolls Royce drove away and the roadsters headed back toward the village."

Had that been a clandestine meeting or had they met by chance? There was still the question of why they had come to this particular village. Again, Evie felt inclined to jump to conclusions and think they had been brought here for a very specific purpose and that meeting had been more than coincidental.

Caro thanked them and they could not have looked more disappointed when she asked them to remain in the house because the detective had everything under control.

"Mariah, is the tea on its way?"

Mariah, who had been hovering near the door, swung around and hurried off to fetch the tea.

"What do you make of that?" Caro asked.

Evie shared her thoughts, adding, "I'm sure Lady McAvoy and her entourage had nothing to do with Mrs. Reid's death but something is definitely going on and Lord Melville is involved."

"What do we do about it?" Tom asked.

She had been engaged to investigate the missing roses. That case had been solved. "Do? The detective is investigating the death. Caro is right. We should stay out of his way. Meanwhile..." Evie smiled, "Caro could entertain us with a performance. Perhaps another scene from Pygmalion."

CHAPTER 21

Curtain call

Caro's enthusiastic performance succeeded in distracting them for a while.

When she finished, Evie and Tom clamored for more. "Encore. Encore. One more scene."

"I'll agree to do one more, but it's the last one." Caro drew in a breath, closed her eyes as if taking a moment to get into character and then recited in a perfect cockney accent, "Y-e-e-e-es, Lord love you! Why should she die of influenza? She come through diphtheria right enough the year before. I saw her with my own eyes. Fairly blue with it, she was. They all thought she was dead; but my father he kept ladling gin down her throat 'til she came to so sudden that she bit the bowl off the spoon."

Showering her with praise, Evie gave her a brilliant smile. "Caro, I believe you have missed your calling."

Belatedly, Evie realized Caro had already displayed her talents when she had played the role of her cousin, thrice removed.

Caro took a bow. As she straightened, a stampede rushed toward the library. At least, it sounded like a stampede. In fact, it was only Mariah running.

She burst through the door and filled the library with a rush of panic and urgency. "Milady, *milady*. The coppers are back."

Caro looked around almost as if searching for a place to hide. "What can the detective possibly want now?" Coming to her senses, she said, "Show the detective in, Mariah." Caro sat down only to jump to her feet again. She moved across to sit opposite Evie and faced the door.

Evie hoped the detective had come to deliver some good news. The sooner he solved the case, the sooner they could all relax.

The detective walked in. He stopped in the middle of the room and fidgeted with the rim of his hat as he said, "Lady Evans, my apologies for bursting in on you again."

Fully composed, Caro gestured to a chair. "That's perfectly fine, detective. How can we help you?"

He acknowledged Evie and Tom and settled down. "I've spoken with Mrs. Higgins and she denied knowing Mrs. Reid. I believe she is prepared to swear it under oath, such is her determination."

Caro stared at the detective, her eyes not blinking. Evie thought she looked thoroughly lost for words, perhaps even confused and she was sure she understood the reason why. Without any effort from them, the detective appeared to have changed his mind about sharing information.

"Do you believe Mrs. Higgins?" Evie asked.

"At this point and, after what you told me earlier today, I can only assume she is lying."

Relieved by his admission, Evie sat back. Now, he would have to find out why Mrs. Higgins had felt it necessary to withhold the information.

"Lady Woodridge, could you perhaps run through what you remember of your encounter with Mrs. Higgins?"

Complying with the detective's request, Evie rummaged through her thoughts and tried to relate what they'd experienced during their brief visit, this time, she tried to be as precise as possible.

To her surprise, the detective took notes and listened without interrupting.

When she finished, she looked to Tom and Caro. "Did I leave anything out?"

They both shook their heads.

Caro looked down at her hands and then exchanged a glance with Tom and Evie. Clearing her throat, she said, "We are actually curious to know how Mrs. Reid died."

Evie thought Caro might be pushing her luck. The detective sat back and avoided making eye contact—an obvious sign of reluctance to share information.

"Detective, I hope you're not trying to spare me the ghastly details. Do I need to remind you I am married to a detective?"

"Very well." He gave her a brisk smile. "At first, it looked as if Mrs. Reid hit her head on a rock. However, even to the untrained eye, the wound didn't look severe enough to cause death. A medical examination revealed bruises on her arm and I have just received an update with the results of the autopsy. Mrs. Reid died of a heart attack." When he finished, he studied their reactions.

"That suggests she died of natural causes." Caro asked the question on everyone's mind, "Could her heart attack have been the result of her encounter?"

The detective looked surprised by Caro's question. "Encounter?"

"We have been considering the possibility Mrs. Reid went out to meet someone. Surely, there must be some sort of sign on the road. The imprint from the tires of a vehicle or footprints. You say she had bruises on her arm. There must be some sign of a struggle."

The detective leaned forward and twirled his pen around. "By the time we arrived, a couple of people had already disturbed the scene. They were farm workers and they said they were walking home from the pub."

Caro looked confused. "At that hour? I thought Mrs. Reid had been found before dawn."

The detective looked down at his hands. "Indeed. Lady Evans, I'm investigating one crime and it's enough that they found the body and reported it."

"Oh, I see. You suspect them of being up to no good."

And he wouldn't question them about their activities, Evie thought as she remembered Louisa mentioning poachers.

"Of course, I am still open to the idea of someone being responsible for her death. However, at this point, we need some solid proof. As I said, we didn't find anything that might have been used as a weapon. On the one hand, it looks as if she might have simply suffered a heart attack and, when she collapsed, she hit her head on a rock. Indeed, there is scientific proof that she died of natural causes. However, one has to ask what she was doing out and about at such a late hour. You're quite correct in thinking the bruises on her arm suggests some sort of argument took place. And that is the reason why I am continuing with my investigation."

"Lady Woodridge considered the possibility of an argument," Tom offered.

"In fact, detective, I thoroughly exhausted the idea."

Looking rather emboldened, Caro said, "I suppose your job now will be to find someone who might have had a motive or reason to argue with Mrs. Reid."

"Indeed. I will now need to carry out a more thorough investigation. That's the reason why I needed to clarify the information you had about Mrs. Higgins." The detective looked at his watch. "But it's late now and I must find lodgings."

"Where will you be staying, detective?" Caro asked. "There is only the pub and they only have one room available. The one occupied by Mrs. Reid. Surely, that won't do."

"I will have to put myself at the mercy of one of the constables."

Caro shook her head. "I know one of them lives in a small cottage." Caro gave it a moment's thought. "You should stay here. Henry would never forgive me if I didn't invite you to stay at Primrose Park."

"My lady, I couldn't impose on you."

When Caro spoke again, Evie forgot she had once been her maid.

"Nonsense. You will stay here." Caro stood up and looked toward the door. "Mariah, could you please make the necessary arrangements? But, before you go, could you help me?"

They both walked into Lord Evans' study.

Evie heard a chair being shifted. Then, Caro and Mariah emerged from the study wheeling out a school blackboard.

"Henry likes to bring his work home. I don't think he'll mind if we use his blackboard."

With the blackboard settled into position, Caro picked up a piece of chalk and began writing.

The detective stood up and went to stand beside Caro, his hands on his hips. She glanced at him and then continued writing.

Evie leaned slightly. With his hands hitched on his hips, the detective's coat had shifted and she thought she could see a shoulder holster.

"Lord Melville?" he asked.

Caro nodded. "He is a viscount and lives…" Caro drew a rough sketch of the village and surrounding estates. "This is where he lives. Where exactly was the body found?"

The detective crossed his arms. Giving a firm nod, he stepped forward and pointed to a spot near a bend leading to Lord Melville's estate.

"I wonder if we can assume she was headed that way. From memory, there is only open countryside beyond that road. Oh, and there's a lodge used for fishing.

According to Mamma, Lord Melville's son, Frederick, stays there when he visits."

"So, there are two possible destinations. Or, maybe three if Mrs. Reid was merely meeting someone on that road," the detective suggested.

Caro turned to the blackboard again. "Motive. We know she visited the village every year. Lady Woodridge suggested looking at the parish registers to establish a relationship with Mrs. Reid and Martha Cooper. Also… Mrs. Higgins' daughter alluded to an ongoing relationship."

"How so?"

"Annabelle thought Mrs. Reid was the woman who occasionally visited Mrs. Higgins. I think we should find out what else Mrs. Reid did during her annual visits to the village."

Frowning, the detective made a few notes—a sign he considered the information worth pursuing.

Evie stood up and stepped forward. "Martha Cooper died twenty-five years ago. I'd like to find out what she did before she died. She might have been married but the headstone doesn't suggest it. We also assume she worked for someone. That information might not help at all. Or, it might draw a clearer picture. It might even be a connection between Mrs. Reid, Martha Cooper and Mrs. Higgins. Who knows? Martha Cooper might have worked for her. Or someone else…"

"Lady Woodridge, are you about to suggest Martha Cooper worked for Lord Melville?"

Evie stepped back. The thought hadn't really occurred to her. Now, more than ever, she thought it would be a good idea to research Martha Cooper's background. "She might have worked for any number of people, including Mrs. Higgins. There's a reason why Mrs. Higgins deliberately changed her tune and denied knowing Mrs. Reid. Caro suggested it could be something insignificant or something so important it would impact her life. What could the association reveal? Heavens…" Evie stopped for a moment as a new thought took shape. "What if there is another crime involved, something that's been hidden for years?" They had recently delved into a death which had been caused by a murder committed in the past.

Evie drew in a deep breath. "Detective, have you spoken with Lord Melville?"

He nodded. "I believe I have spoken with the majority of villagers. Lord Melville had guests for dinner and they left rather late."

"How late?"

"Well after midnight."

"And, have you established a specific time of death?"

"Sometime after midnight." He looked uncertain for a moment and then added, "Lord Melville claims he retired straight after his guests left."

How could they confirm that?

"And his word is good enough for you?"

"Lady Woodridge, I would need to have some solid proof of wrongdoing before accusing Lord Melville of lying."

"Because he is a peer?" Evie huffed.

The detective did not answer.

Everyone fell silent and looked at the blackboard.

Evie knew she would spend the night tossing and

turning and trying to figure out how Lord Melville could have left his house to meet Mrs. Reid.

After a moment, Evie spoke up. "Detective, have you spoken with Lady McAvoy and her entourage? From what I understand, they traveled along that road. I find it hard to believe they didn't see anything."

The detective sighed. "They were too inebriated to have seen anything. In fact, I'm surprised they made it back to their lodgings unscathed. I'm afraid this is not going to be easy. The villain in this story will not be revealed by a close in on his black moustache and shiny black top hat."

"I'm happy to investigate Lady Woodridge's idea," Caro said. "In fact, I'm suddenly suspicious of everyone in this entire village. They might all be party to a secret which has been kept hidden for many years."

The sonorous sound of a gong caught them all by surprise.

Caro looked puzzled and glanced at the clock on the mantle. "I suppose that's the dressing gong." Gesturing to the footman standing at the door, Caro said, "Steven will show you to your room."

When the detective left, Caro murmured, "Steven looked rather pleased. I believe that's the first time he's rang the dressing gong since I arrived."

Evie patted her shoulder. "Caro, servants are becoming increasingly more difficult to replace. You should try to keep him happy. I daresay, you have your work cut out for you."

Caro could not have looked more horrified. "Are you suggesting I need to start entertaining? I've just declared the entire village suspects in a murder investigation. If word gets out, I will be ostracized."

Knowing how she felt about mingling with the local gentry, Evie smiled. "They won't find out."

Caro lowered her voice. "You'd think it would be easy to find someone who wasn't where they were supposed to be. This is a small village. I'm sure everyone knows everyone's business."

Being a small village, Evie thought, most people would depend on large estates for their livelihood. If someone had seen Lord Melville out and about in the middle of the night, would they remain loyal to him, or would they report the activity to the police? "During dinner we should try to make sure the detective has spoken to everyone within the vicinity of the village. No stone left unturned."

"I thought you'd be more interested in focusing on Lord Melville." Caro's cheeks reddened. "I didn't care for his alibi or the fact that he received preferential treatment because of his title."

"Lord Melville has made himself a target. Apart from us, he appears to be the only other person who's shown an interest in the case. I'm sure the detective will find a way to continue investigating him until he finds solid proof." Evie brightened. "Perhaps we can call on him. Who knows, he might let something slip."

CHAPTER 22

The next morning
Primrose Park

Evie made her way down to the dining room and found Caro and Tom just settling down to their breakfast. "Has the mail arrived?" She and Tom had only been away for a couple of days but she had assumed Henrietta or Toodles would have written by now.

"Yes. I received a letter from my mother. She will be visiting next month. That will keep me on my toes."

"And what about the detective? Has he left already?"

"No, he came in for some coffee and now he's in the library. I believe he is studying the blackboard. I find myself agreeing with Mamma. He can't possibly function on an empty stomach. I will ask Mrs. Haighs to prepare a small basket of food for him to take on his travels." Caro looked over the rim of her cup. "I only hope I didn't scare him away with my silly acting."

The previous evening, she and Tom had requested yet another performance from Caro and had found it just as entertaining as her other performances. "Caro, it was divine and the detective thoroughly enjoyed himself. I saw him smiling and laughing. And that's probably why he's now eager to get to work. You cleared his mind and offered him a distraction he obviously needed."

Evie sat down opposite Caro who held up a newspaper. Reading the headline, Evie grimaced. "Death has come to Primrose. I hope the article is more reassuring."

"Just barely." Caro shook her head. "I don't understand why journalists need to sensationalize the news. It makes people uneasy. I'm sure Mariah slept with a chair lodged against the door."

Tom looked up from his breakfast. "Do we have a plan for today?"

"We could go on a carriage ride," Evie suggested. "I haven't stopped thinking about it since Caro mentioned it. Or, you could give Caro some driving lessons. Then again, Caro might have something planned for us."

"I'm afraid not. Is that a sign of a bad hostess?"

Tom laughed. "You just missed your opportunity to say you went to a lot of trouble to plan a murder for Evie."

Caro grinned. "I didn't want to be too obvious."

Evie buttered her toast. "Well, I'm sure we can find something entertaining to do."

"Countess, does that mean you don't wish to continue with the investigation? What's come over you? I assumed you'd want to shadow the detective's every step."

"Only if he invites us to do so." Caro had been in two minds about snooping around and she didn't want to add to her confusion or distress.

Caro took a sip of her coffee and added another spoonful of sugar. "What about the parish records? Please tell me we are going to look at them today. I spent the entire night thinking about them."

"I'm sure the detective will get around to visiting the vicar." After dinner, they had spent some time going through everything they'd seen and heard again and the possibility of underlying connections had been discussed at length.

"But it won't be the same. You see things in a different way." Caro looked worried. "Have you lost interest in becoming a lady detective?"

No, she hadn't. "I wasn't sure how you felt, especially as it means going out and mingling with the locals. I know I forced you to attend the garden party…"

"Oh, never mind all that. Mamma is right. It wouldn't hurt to be seen out and about with you."

Evie accepted the compliment with a smile. After a moment, she frowned. "Is that because I represent all that is respectable or because I have a reputation for becoming mixed up in murder investigations and, if word gets out about you suspecting the villagers, you can blame it on me?"

Caro looked rather pleased. "I believe that is called killing two birds with one stone."

"Fine, I don't mind serving a purpose… or two. We'll pay the vicar a visit."

Mariah walked in and had a whispered conversation with Caro.

Looking surprised, Caro announced, "It seems the constables just arrived and alerted the detective to a new development and he has now left." Turning back to Mariah, Caro asked, "Did you happen to overhear anything?"

"No, milady. But the coppers appeared to be eager to give chase."

They all wondered what that might be about.

"I suppose we'll find out about it sooner or later. Meanwhile, the way is clear for us to set off. Here's an idea. After we talk with the vicar, we could pay Lord Melville a visit and then we can compare notes with the detective."

Caro looked positively mortified by the idea. "How? Why? I mean… How do we justify our visit?"

"We could say we were curious to know if the detective had called on him."

"Lord Melville is not going to like it. Yesterday, he didn't even make eye contact with me."

"Caro, he ignored everyone but Louisa. We can at least trust him to remain true to his nature. But the man is hiding something."

~

Meanwhile…
Halton House

. . .

Millicent peered inside a large vase. She had been inspecting every decorative vase at Halton House, looking for the mangled cushions she had hidden and had, so far, failed to find a single one.

Had someone else found them?

Grumbling, she looked at Holmes. "Is it that we don't feed you enough?"

"Millicent?"

Millicent jumped back.

Edgar!

Fixing a smile in place, she turned. "Edgar."

He approached her, his upright manner softening slightly. "Has Master Holmes been giving you trouble?"

"N-no. Not really."

"Don't you think you should put him down. It seems that every time I see you, you're holding him in your arms. He is a puppy and needs exercise."

Could that be the problem with Holmes? What if she played a game with him? Growing up, her parents had kept a goat and a cow for milk, but no dogs so she had no idea how to entertain one. She knew Holmes had enjoyed it when she'd chased after him in the village…

Edgar looked over his shoulder. Turning back to her, he lowered his voice, "How are you getting on with Eliza Barton? I've noticed you don't converse with her in the dining room."

Millicent lifted her chin. She hadn't told Edgar about her suspicions yet. It seemed every time she tried, she succumbed to a sense of dread. What if he thought her silly and even, perhaps, a tiny bit jealous of the new secretary?

They had a solid relationship and she didn't want it ruined by something that might come to nothing. She didn't want to admit it, but she might be wrong about Eliza Barton.

"We're getting along just fine. You seem to forget I'm her ladyship's maid now. I have to behave with more decorum."

He studied her for a moment and then nodded. "By the way, we seem to be missing a cushion from the library. It's one embroidered by Lady Henrietta. Have you seen it?"

Holmes barked and wagged his tail.

"I'm sure it's around... somewhere."

Primrose Village

Deciding to try their luck with the vicar first, Tom found a spot for the motor car and they set off toward the church on foot.

The roadsters belonging to the bright young things were nowhere to be seen. Evie noticed a couple of villagers turning to look at them. By now, everyone would have read the newspaper headlines. The thought reminded her of the photograph which had appeared in a New York newspaper. She hadn't received any mail from home so she assumed the journalists and photographers had not yet descended on Halton House. In any case, they would soon lose interest because, of course, she wasn't there.

For a split second, Evie pictured Henrietta and Toodles taking the situation in hand and dealing with the intrusion in their own unique way. Before she could dismiss the idea, a thought took shape and she imagined them engaging the servants to dress up as the Countess of Woodridge and Mr. Tom Winchester…

Fortunately, something caught her attention.

"Oh, is that Annabelle Higgins?" Evie asked and pointed to a young woman coming out of a store.

Caro squinted. "It looks like her."

"She's not alone." A young boy rushed out of the store and caught up with Annabelle who patted him on the head. When she headed toward them, Evie smiled and greeted her.

"Lady Woodridge." She seemed surprised to see them.

"Hello, Annabelle." Evie looked down at the young boy and smiled at him.

Annabelle put her arm around her young companion. "This is my brother, Jason."

He could not have been more than ten years old, Evie thought. "How is your dear mother?"

Annabelle's cheeks colored. "She is keeping busy with her garden." Looking around her, she gave Evie a brisk smile. "I… I should hurry. We are expected back home."

Evie watched her walk away. "She seemed to be eager to get away."

"I wouldn't be surprised if Mrs. Higgins told her to keep her distance from us," Caro said. "If Annabelle knows something, we won't be able to question her."

Evie found herself wondering about the obvious age

difference between the siblings. "How old do you think her brother is?"

"No more than ten, I'm sure."

"Countess, why are we lingering?" Tom asked, his attention fixed on the dowager's house down the street.

"Tom's right. We should hurry. We don't want to miss the vicar again."

They found the vicar talking with a parishioner outside the church. Evie felt an instant sense of disappointment. He looked too young. Mrs. Reid's sister, Martha Cooper, had died twenty-five years ago. Too long ago for him to have been around. She could only hope they would find some valuable information in the parish records.

Mrs. Reid's annual pilgrimage to visit her sister's grave suggested a strong bond had existed between them. However, Evie suspected there might have been another reason for her visits.

Had Mrs. Reid known other villagers? When had she moved away? "We should have asked the barkeeper about Mrs. Reid's stay at the pub. I wouldn't mind knowing if she made a habit of visiting for several days or just the one day."

"Perhaps Mamma's maid will be able to tell us."

"How old do you think the vicar is?" Evie laughed under her breath. "My apologies, I seem to be relying on you to estimate people's ages. I'm afraid I've never been a good judge."

Caro studied him for a moment. "I'm trying to look past his youthful looks. Some men can grow old, yet still retain their boyish looks."

As he spoke, the vicar's shoulders stooped slightly and he appeared to be making himself smaller to match the parishioner's shorter height. He smiled, not just with his lips but also with his eyes, making him instantly likeable.

Finally, he shook hands with the woman who then walked off with a slight spring to her step.

Despite having given all his attention to the parishioner, he must have noticed them hovering nearby. Giving them an acknowledging nod, he took a step toward them.

Evie homed in on his welcoming smile. It almost felt like an embrace.

Caro, who had already met the vicar, introduced him. "This is the Reverend Richard Lander." Wasting no time, she then explained their interest in Martha Cooper.

The vicar gave a slow shake of his head. "Such sad news about Mrs. Reid."

"You knew her?" Evie asked.

"Oh, yes. I met her soon after I arrived. This would have been just before the war. An amiable woman with an interest in all the parishioners. She always visited her sister's grave when she arrived in the village and when she left."

They had been related!

At least, they now had solid confirmation.

He guided them to his office and, after a search through a large bookcase, he produced one of the registers.

The family had lived in the area for several generations. They had married, baptized their children and been buried here.

Unfortunately, the vicar had not lived in the area long enough to know anything other than factual information.

Evie insisted Mrs. Reid's visits were not merely about paying her respects. There had to have been an underlying reason hidden somewhere.

The vicar pushed his spectacles back. "There is something…" Looking toward the bookcase, he gave a pensive nod. "My predecessor kept a journal. In fact, there are several boxes of them. When I found them, I tried to locate any family members who might be interested in them as a keepsake. Unfortunately, no one wanted them. I haven't had the heart to dispose of them. I remember looking through one and it contained ruminations as well as snippets of his encounters with his parishioners, also…" He looked down and a hint of a blush colored his cheeks. "Some might call it gossip."

Yes, but did the journals go back far enough.

Evie expressed a keen interest in seeing them and wondered if he might allow them to look through them.

"I don't see any harm in it, but what do you hope to find in them?"

"We don't really know."

They spent the next hour searching through the boxes and reading journals written over the years and stretching back to the time of Martha Cooper's death. However, they didn't find any direct mention of Martha Cooper.

Caro set one journal down and flicked through another one. "I doubt this will have anything. He wrote it a while after she died." Then she sat back and read through a page. When she reached the end, she turned the page. "This might be something. The vicar refers to someone by her initials. M.C. It might be Martha Cooper."

"What does he say?" Evie asked.

"M.C. died in childbirth."

CHAPTER 23

*E*vie avoided becoming too excited. Once again, they had a snippet of information but not exactly a solid lead. Certainly not something they could present to the detective.

With the vicar's permission, they took the journal with them, saying they wished to show it to the detective.

"What if he'd said no?" Tom asked as they made their way out.

Evie hummed as she considered the question. "I wonder if I would have had the courage to create a distraction so that one of you could steal it?"

Tom's step faltered. "Ask a simple question and, suddenly, Caro and I are enlisted to commit theft. Countess, you're becoming a bad influence."

"All for the greater good," Evie assured him. "If we don't find anything of interest in this journal, we might need to go through the rest."

"That's fine by me," Tom said. "Just so long as you

don't expect us to break into the vicarage in the middle of the night to steal them."

"Good heavens. I made a speculative suggestion and, suddenly, I am perceived as a criminal mastermind."

"I suppose all criminals need to start somewhere," Caro jested.

They walked back along the main street. Despite the detective carrying out his investigation, the villagers appeared to have resumed their everyday lives. Evie noticed only one person turning as they walked by, but they were not the man's target as he appeared to have forgotten something.

Caro turned to Evie. "Do you think we have developed an appetite for terrible deeds? The reason I ask is because I haven't really given any thought to how I feel about my interest in criminal activities and I wonder if it's something I have always been interested in. My mother still enjoys reading the penny dreadful stories she inherited from her mother and, I must admit, I have read every single story in her collection."

"I grew up reading those dime novels but I didn't develop an obsession with murder. Actually, I wish they'd prepared me for the reality of crimes. But they didn't. I must admit I occasionally entertain a few doubts about my involvement."

Tom held the passenger door open for them. "You now seem to be quite prepared to tackle this mystery. I've yet to hear you suggest contacting Lotte Mannering or your new secretary."

Caro looked surprised. "Secretary? How does Millicent feel about that?"

"I doubt Millicent has given it much thought. She is over the moon happy with her new lady's maid position. Anyway, I'm sure she and Eliza Barton are now steadfast friends."

Tom explained, "Before we left Halton House, Evie made sure everyone felt comfortable with the new secretary. This time, when we return, there'll be no surprises waiting for us. At least, that's the plan."

"The roadsters are not here. I wonder if that means the bright young things have left?" Their presence in the village still bothered Evie. "We identified the people responsible for stealing the roses and yet I don't feel entirely satisfied."

"Nor do I," Caro said. "In fact, I believe the detective was too quick to dismiss them as possible suspects. If Lady Henrietta had been here, she would have demanded he lock them up for a day or two to make them talk."

As they made their way to Lord Melville's estate, Evie tried to formulate a few questions they could use to lead him to reveal something he had withheld from the detective. Caro had been right to suggest that even if Lord Melville provided the same information, she might be able to read something else between the lines.

Lost in her thoughts, Evie did not see the motor car heading toward them until Tom slowed down.

They had turned into the narrow road leading to the estate and Evie could see one of the two motor cars would have to give way.

Caro hunched forward. "It looks like he is determined to have the right of way."

Tom steered the vehicle onto the shoulder and stopped.

"Actually, he might have other intentions," Tom muttered. "He's headed straight for us."

Instead of driving by, the motor car came to a sudden stop. A man climbed out. He wore a brown suit and a cap and he held something in his hands.

Caro's voice hitched, "Is that a cricket bat? He looks like he means business."

The man stomped toward them but Tom didn't give him the opportunity to reach them. Jumping out of the car, he matched him stride for stride.

The man's shoulders looked tense with aggression, while Tom remained relaxed.

"Good heavens," Caro exclaimed. "Are they going to fight? Should we do something?" She looked around the motor car.

"Caro, are you looking for something to use as a weapon?"

"Yes."

Thinking it might actually be a good idea, Evie grabbed her handbag and tested it for weight and sturdiness. "I believe we are quite defenseless."

"What do we do?" Caro reached for the door handle with one hand and wrapped her other hand around Evie's arm.

They both stared at the two men confronting each other.

Tom had his hands spread out in front of him. Evie worried the other man might perceive it as an aggressive move instead of a placating gesture.

When she sensed Caro turning the door handle, Evie grabbed hold of Caro's hand and tugged her back. "I think it might be best to stay out of it."

"I prefer the odds of three against one," Caro argued.

"Tom can handle himself," Evie assured her even as she reached for the door handle.

"Well, I wish he'd hurry up about it. I don't like the look of this."

The man swung his bat onto his shoulder.

Evie and Caro gasped.

Still holding on to each other's hand, they both tried to open their respective doors and climb out only to spring back as they pulled themselves back inside.

Caro groaned. "You're right. We should stay out of the way."

They both stared straight ahead.

Confronted with the threat of a cricket bat, Tom lowered his hands and hitched them on his waist. A second later, the man's cricket bat lowered and dropped. He bent down to pick it up, swung away and climbed into his motor car.

Tom remained standing there until the would-be assailant drove away. Then, he turned and, looking relaxed again, he walked toward them.

Caro scooped in a breath. "What just happened?"

Evie supposed they'd have to wait for Tom to explain. When he drew nearer, she could see his jaw muscles twitching. She had no trouble imagining him grinding his back teeth together.

He climbed in and leaned on his seat to look at them. "What are you two doing?"

They were still holding each other's hand.

"We were going to rescue you," Caro said. "At least, we were going to make a brave attempt to rescue you."

"Who was he?" Evie asked. "And what did he want?"

"He wanted us to leave." Tom straightened. After a moment, he said, "Lord Melville's chauffeur is rather territorial."

"His chauffeur?"

Tom nodded. "He felt rather strongly about us being here."

"And how did you dissuade him?"

"I employed reason," he clipped out. "Anyhow, in the end, he was actually rather helpful. He told me Lord Melville is doing a spot of fishing by the river near the fishing lodge. Shall we proceed?"

As they continued along the narrow road, Evie exchanged a look with Caro that spoke of curiosity. They'd only seen the back of Tom. Whatever he'd said had clearly been enough to discourage the chauffeur from using his cricket bat.

Caro pointed ahead. "The river is on the right-hand side and I think that road might lead to it."

"There's only one way to find out." Slowing down, Tom made the turn but when the road became too uneven to navigate, Tom stopped. "Ladies, I believe we'll have to walk the rest of the way."

They walked through a wooded area, following a well-trodden path. Coming up to a clearing, they saw the river and Lord Melville standing on the bank, a fishing rod in hand.

"He cuts a lonely figure," Evie observed.

"He's fishing," Tom said, his tone matter of fact.

Evie glanced at Tom and waited for him to say more. "I take it fishing is a lonely activity. I've never thought about it that way. I've had the most entertaining conversations while fishing."

"That's your opinion." Tom smiled at her. "Did you ever ask how the other person felt?"

Evie tilted her head and returned the smile. "We've never been fishing together. Do you enjoy it?"

"I've only ever gone fishing when I've had to find my next meal."

"I take it this was during your wildcatter days."

"If I could interrupt for a moment," Caro said. "Are we going to talk with Lord Melville or not?"

They emerged onto the clearing and walked toward Lord Melville. Sensing them, he turned and looked away only to do a double-take.

"I guess we are the last people he expected to see here," Evie said.

His fishing rod lowered and he stilled.

Evie murmured, "He's probably debating whether or not to use our formal titles." Smiling, Evie walked toward him. "Lord Melville. I hope we are not interrupting your fishing."

Lifting his chin, he gave her a measuring look. Evie imagined him thinking she had quite the audacity to approach him. No doubt, he had also dismissed her as a *parvenu*.

"Lady Woodridge. Not at all. I'm afraid they're not biting today but I'm not prepared to abandon all hope just yet." He glanced at Caro and Tom. "Lady Evans and Mr. Winchester. Are you all out for a stroll?"

"Yes, it's such a lovely day," Evie offered. On the way here, she'd tried to come up with a credible excuse for calling on him, but had drawn a blank. Then, right from out of nowhere, she plucked out an idea. "We actually ended up here because we were following Lady McAvoy and her entourage. We were sure we saw them headed this way."

His jaw set and his lips firmed.

Evie continued, spinning the tale further, "They sped away but I swear they turned into the road leading to your estate."

"Why would they do that?" he asked even as he turned away.

He hadn't asked who Lady McAvoy was or even denied knowing her, something Evie found quite interesting.

"Oh, we assumed she knows you or your son."

Lord Melville swung toward Evie. She had trouble understanding how he saw anything, holding his head up as he did.

"I doubt my son knows Lady McAvoy even exists." His manner changed from snobbish to curious. "Come to think of it, I might have seen Lady McAvoy and her lot at Mrs. Higgins' garden party."

"Yes, you probably did. That's where we first saw them. Anyhow, despite losing them, we continued on in the hope that we might find you. And, here we are. You see… we have also been curious to know if the detective caught up with you."

"He did indeed." Lord Melville gave the reel a couple of turns and then stopped. "I suppose the fellow has a job to do. I'm afraid I couldn't be of much help."

Evie couldn't think of any reason to ask, but she couldn't resist... "Did he ask you about Martha Cooper?"

Lord Melville stilled. "Why would he? I didn't know her."

Evie realized he hadn't offered the denial she'd expected. "But you're familiar with the name."

He made a dismissive gesture with his hand. With a shake of his head, he resumed reeling in his line. "I'm sure I've heard the name mentioned somewhere. I assume she's a villager."

"She was Mrs. Reid's sister."

"The woman who died?"

"Yes, I assume you knew her."

"Why would you assume that?"

"Oh, I'm sure someone mentioned seeing you talking with her."

"What utter nonsense," he sputtered.

His fishing rod curved slightly and the line tightened. He gave it an impatient tug, but the line appeared to be stuck. Muttering under his breath, he dug inside his pocket, drew out a knife and cut the line. "Well, that's that."

He fumbled with his pocket, something Evie had seen him do at the dowager's house. Then he checked his pocket watch.

"I didn't realize it was so late. I'm afraid I must be going now."

Abandoning his fishing gear, presumably for someone

else to collect, he turned and left, disappearing into a wooded area.

"I wonder if he realizes he just became a real person of interest."

"I'm sorry I couldn't be of any help," Caro said. "I couldn't think of anything to ask him. In fact, I struggled to follow your line of questioning."

"I just wanted him to admit to knowing Martha Cooper."

Caro looked confused. "I'm embarrassed to admit it, but I'm not sure why we are interested in Mrs. Reid's sister. I know we're hoping to find something in the vicar's journal but I'm not clear about what we're looking for."

Evie tried to remember her reasoning. "I'm not sure either. Other family members are buried in the churchyard. Yet, Mrs. Reid only showed an interest in her sister's grave."

"Maybe they had a close relationship." Caro shrugged. "It's possible Mrs. Reid never came to terms with her loss."

"That's an interesting observation, Caro."

"Oh, yes. I suddenly understand our interest in her sister."

"Do you remember what Louisa's maid said? It's that time of year and Martha Cooper has flowers again. She might have said Mrs. Reid is visiting her family or some such thing, but she didn't." Evie gave a determined shake of her head. "Mrs. Reid was making a point with her visits. I think we should return to Primrose Park and dive into that journal. Tom? Caro? Do you have any other ideas?"

Caro nibbled the edge of her lip. "You're right in suspecting him. Lord Melville is definitely worried about something. He was as evasive as Mrs. Higgins... You might be in the process of uncovering an old secret."

Evie hadn't thought about it along those lines. "Now I'd like to know when Mrs. Reid left the village." She'd been born here and had, most likely, worked here. Why had she left?

As they made their way back to the motor car, Evie said, "The detective is investigating Mrs. Reid's death. However, I think he needs to dig around and get all the information he can about her sister. I believe she might hold the key to something significant."

CHAPTER 24

Primrose Park

Mariah must have been watching out for them. The moment they drove into Primrose Park, she and the footmen emerged from the house.

"Milady, we didn't expect you back so soon. Would you like me to tell Mrs. Haighs to prepare luncheon?"

"Yes, please, Mariah. Meanwhile, we'd love some tea. Bring it to the library, please."

Walking inside the house, Caro whispered, "I'm not sure why both footmen came out. Do you think they're desperate to do something?"

"I'm sure they'll be run off their feet in no time, Caro. You shouldn't fret."

"You seem to forget I worked in service. I know what happens when the servants have nothing to do."

"I promise Tom and I will visit you often. That should keep them busy until you find your feet."

"I'm actually worried they'll start acting like the Halton House servants."

Good heavens, Evie thought. Suddenly, she worried about what she and Tom would be returning to.

Lost in her thoughts, she fell behind and had to hurry to join the others as they made their way to the library.

Moments later, she managed to lose herself in the contents of the journal.

Mariah walked in and set a tray on a small table.

Evie looked up and accepted a cup of tea. "Let he who is without sin cast the first stone," she read. "The vicar goes on to say one person's misfortune is another person's longed for gift. What could that mean?"

"I hope the vicar didn't mean to imply M.C.'s death was something desired by someone else." Shuddering, Caro set her cup down and turned to look at the blackboard. "Should we add her to the list, just in case?"

"Perhaps wait until we know more."

They knew M.C. had died in childbirth. While the entry had been written several months after Martha Cooper's death, they had no way of knowing if the vicar had been referring to Martha Cooper, but they couldn't ignore the possibility.

"What do people long for?" Evie asked, mostly because she didn't wish to blurt out the obvious answer. Instead, she wanted to see if there were alternatives she hadn't thought about.

Caro suggested, "Rest. Tranquility. After the havoc of the last few years, definitely peace. The bright young things would say they spent the war years longing for fun."

Evie read the passage again and said, "I had a relative who married young and spent her life longing for a child."

"My mother longed for her first child," Caro said. "Then, the rest came along and not a day went by when she didn't shake her head at the mischief my brothers and I would get up to. However, yes, people long for children."

"I wonder what happened to M.C.'s baby." Also, if they scoured through the parish registers, would they be able to identify M.C.? "Would there be a record of a family member taking the child?"

Evie brushed her fingertips along the page. She understood why the vicar had used initials. Reading the following passages, it became clear the vicar had been ruminating over the misfortune befalling some young women.

M.C. had not been married so her baby had been born out of wedlock.

"Hypothetically," Evie continued, "if M.C. stands for Martha Cooper, perhaps Mrs. Reid took the baby. There's no mention of it here. But there must be a record of the christening. We'll definitely have to look through the parish registers again."

Tom reached for the journal and sat back to read through it. "This entry was written nearly a year after Martha Cooper's death. The local doctor's records—"

"Of course," Caro chirped. "Why didn't it occur to us before? That's one way to find out how Martha Cooper died. And, if she died in childbirth, then we can assume M.C. is Martha Cooper with more certainty."

A thought began to take shape in her mind. Evie sat back to ponder it.

Tom closed the journal. "Since we know M.C. wasn't married... Oh..."

"What?" Evie sat up.

"I'm entertaining a possibility and I'm suddenly reminded of the times you do the same. The thought is taking shape in my mind but it sounds incredibly farfetched."

Evie looked at Caro and they both nodded.

"We'd still like to hear it, please. In any case, I'm entertaining my own theory but it refuses to take shape."

"Well, there must be a father somewhere and I'm willing to bet he still lives in the village. And... Yes, even without absolute proof, I'm willing to bet M.C. is Martha Cooper."

"In that case, we must definitely find out where Martha Cooper worked before she died. That might lead us to him," Evie suggested.

Caro gasped. "Are you thinking she might have worked for one of the large estates and the lord of the manor might have been responsible for getting her pregnant?" Caro jumped to her feet and approached the blackboard. She wrote down Martha Cooper's name and drew an arrow.

"Lord Melville?"

Caro nodded and swung around. "That would give him motive for murder."

Evie's eyebrows shot up.

"Yes, I know, in one breath I've accused him of seducing a servant and killing a woman. But what if Mrs.

Reid knew. Or... Or maybe she'd had her suspicions and, after all these years, she finally decided to confront Lord Melville and accuse him of ruining her sister."

"Good heavens. You're right. And maybe that's why Mrs. Reid kept coming back year after year. She was probably searching for clues."

Caro stepped back from the blackboard. "I have another theory. What if she knew all along. You were right to want to know more about their backgrounds. What if Mrs. Reid had been in service right here in the village and, suddenly, after her sister's death, she moved away and never had to work a day in her life again."

"How would she have accomplished that?" Evie asked.

"Blackmail." Caro held up a finger. "This isn't such a wild supposition. Remember what Mamma's maid said about seeing Lord Melville arguing with Mrs. Reid. Think about it. Mrs. Reid spent all these years blackmailing him and, suddenly, something changes, she demands more money and if he doesn't deliver, she threatens to expose him as the immoral man that he is. They meet in the darkness of night and he... Well, he does something or other to cause her heart attack. He claims to have an alibi because he entertained his guests until after midnight. But, after that, he would have been free to sneak out of the house to meet her."

Evie and Tom surged to their feet.

"We should tell the detective but, before we do, we should make sure we have the correct information. What if Louisa's maid made a mistake about seeing Lord Melville arguing with a woman? We need to speak with Louisa's maid."

Tom rolled his eyes. "Yes, I'm perfectly fine with paying Louisa a visit."

"But first, we must visit the doctor. Caro is right. We should have thought of that first."

They all turned to leave only to stop when the library door opened.

The detective walked in. "Your maid said you'd be here."

"Detective. We were just on our way out…"

"Please don't let me stop you, my lady."

"Oh, dear… I've just realized Mrs. Haighs is preparing luncheon." Looking at the others, Caro added, "A slight delay won't matter, will it?"

Trying their best to hide their disappointment, Tom and Evie stepped back and returned to their chairs.

The detective went to stand in front of the blackboard. "M.C.?"

Tom produced the journal. "We have been following a possible lead, detective." He explained the rest of their theory. "Of course, it might come to nothing."

The detective gestured to the journal. "May I?"

"Certainly." Tom handed it to him.

After reading through it, the detective looked up. "It's odd. I'm actually beginning to see a connection where I would never have imagined one existed before."

By odd, did he mean he didn't usually accept unsolicited opinions or consider them of any worth?

Caro stepped forward. "Detective, I hope you will join us for luncheon. And, that reminds me. This morning you rushed off without having any breakfast. It must have been quite urgent."

"Oh, yes... There was some trouble with Lady McAvoy's group."

Surprised, Caro gasped. "They're still here? What did they do this time?"

"This time?" The detective set the journal aside. "Is there something you forgot to mention, my lady?"

"Oh... I... I'm sure I told you about it. In any case, it's really nothing."

His eyebrow hitched up.

"So... what sort of trouble did they create?" Caro asked again.

"They smashed one of their roadsters into a farm gate and the livestock escaped from the pasture." He looked at Evie. "Lady Woodridge, should I find that suspicious?"

"I'm not sure what you mean?"

He gestured to the journal. "You seem to have a knack for unearthing interesting scraps of information."

Deciding he had meant to pay her a compliment, Evie shrugged. "And yet, you still haven't apprehended the culprit."

The footman entered the library and stood by the door. Caro took that as a signal. "I believe luncheon is ready."

Making up for his missed breakfast, the detective enjoyed a hearty meal but still managed to focus on Evie's abilities to dig up leads. "When I arrived, were you about to follow a new lead?"

"We were simply eager to paint a full picture of Mrs. Reid," Evie answered. "We feel that the more we know about her, the more chances we'll have of finding a possible motive."

"Perhaps I can help with that," he offered.

He had everyone's attention.

The detective took a sip of wine and then proceeded to tell them the following, "She worked as a housemaid for a country solicitor right here in the village. When she married, she moved to Birmingham. She'd been a widow for ten years. We know she visited her sister's grave every year right from the start so her changed circumstances did not trigger it. From that, we can also reach a similar conclusion and say no other event triggered her visits to the village. She always stayed for three days and then returned home. During her stay, she would visit with several of the villagers. I've spoken with all of them but they had nothing to contribute."

Evie expected him to refer to his notebook, but he didn't. "How did you learn all that?"

"The police, as you must surely know, have the authority to question suspects and persons of interest. I assume you are employing unusual, creative and, dare I say, unorthodox tactics to get information. I have to wonder what else you might have discovered."

Seeing Evie hesitating, Caro offered, "Lord Melville knew Martha Cooper because… he didn't categorically deny it."

The detective smiled at Caro. "I should hate to fall foul of your particular brand of investigative tactics, my lady. But you are quite right. I found Lord Melville in every way as evasive as Mrs. Higgins has been to date." He turned to Evie, his raised eyebrow prompting her to answer his earlier question.

Evie arranged a piece of carrot next to a pea and added

some beef to the combination. "Our theories might gain more credibility if we could confirm a few more details."

"Such as?"

Evie glanced at his coat pocket. They were still enjoying their meal so she couldn't really expect him to take notes.

Yet, he did.

Drawing out his notebook, he set it on the table and opened it to a clean page.

"You found out all you could about Mrs. Reid but what about her sister?" Evie set her fork down. "I've just remembered a thought that had started to take shape earlier today. Martha Cooper's baby." Evie reminded him of their theory about M.C. actually being Martha Cooper. "We need to know what happened to the baby. Did someone adopt it. Since you didn't mention it, we have to discount the possibility Mrs. Reid took the baby. That begs the question. Why didn't she?"

"The promise of a better life," he suggested. "Or, she might not have known the fate of the baby."

"There is someone in the village who has drawn my attention. Annabelle. Did you know she has a younger brother?"

"No, I didn't."

"We estimate there is at least a fifteen-year age difference. That is quite significant, but not entirely unheard of. I have a relative who had a child at twenty, another one at thirty and her last one at forty. I've also heard of women who experience difficulties at first. They then adopt a child and then, several years later, they are surprised by the arrival of their own child. What if…" Evie drew in a breath and reconsidered her question only to blurt it out, "What if Mrs. Higgins is not Annabelle's natural mother?"

The detective sat back. "That would explain her behavior." He made a note of it. "So, assuming M.C. is Martha Cooper, you think Mrs. Higgins took the baby. She would definitely want to keep that a secret."

"Oh, dear. I'm afraid you will now have to look into Mrs. Higgins' past. Where was she twenty-five years ago? Did she live in the village then? I'm not suggesting Mrs. Higgins is responsible for causing Mrs. Reid's heart attack. But… Well, if she had been living here, she might have taken the baby with or without the consent of Martha Cooper's surviving relative."

He dabbed the edge of his mouth with his napkin and stood up. "If you'll excuse me…" The detective picked up his notebook and left in a hurry.

One by one they turned their attention to their meals. After a moment, Caro spoke up, "Mrs. Reid is rather fortunate to have us. The police don't always have the resources to launch an investigation and rely heavily on the amount of evidence they can acquire in order to decide if they'll proceed. The autopsy results might have been enough to close the case and declare it a death by natural causes. I hope she gets justice."

"Well said, Caro. Seen from that perspective, I feel our meddling has been justified. Although, I trust the detective would have found something suspicious about the death to justify investigating further."

Mariah peered in. Noticing this, Caro asked, "What is it, Mariah?"

The housemaid stepped forward. "I've been trying to

find the right time, milady, but if I wait, I'm afraid it will be too late."

Caro encouraged her with a nod.

"One of the footmen, I won't say which one it was, overheard the conversation you were having about Martha Cooper's place of employment." Mariah gave a firm nod, almost as if she'd just given herself permission to continue. "Well, I can tell you with absolute certainty something which was relayed to me by someone whose name I don't wish to mention…"

"Mariah." Caro's tone carried a degree of warning, suggesting Mariah should simply come out with it.

"She had been in service at Lord Melville's estate. By she, I don't mean the cat's mother, I mean Martha Cooper."

"Truly? Mariah, how do you know this?"

Mariah lifted her chin. "I cannot, in good conscience, reveal my sources. All I can say is that I… I asked someone, I won't mention the person's name, but she is old enough to have been around at the time."

Evie wondered if Mariah had spoken with the cook, Mrs. Haighs.

"Why didn't you say something before?" Caro asked.

Mariah gave an insouciant shrug. "I don't make a habit of eavesdropping on your conversations, milady. And, if you recall, the footmen have been otherwise engaged. Now, they are back and can serve as my eyes and ears. I mean… not that I've asked them to. One of them only now heard the conversation but he didn't want to be the one to tell you."

They all turned to the footman.

He stared straight ahead, his eyes not even blinking.

"Better late than never, Mariah. Thank you."

They finished their meal in silence and decided to take a short walk around the estate to mull over what they now knew.

"What's on your mind, Countess?"

"I'm considering a highly unorthodox method. We should try confronting Lord Melville." Evie looked up. "Will someone please talk me out of it? Common sense tells me we should wait for the detective." She walked on and stopped. "Oh, dear. We forgot to tell the detective about the doctor. I'm sure we forgot. By the time he returns, it will probably be too late in the day and we'll have to wait until tomorrow."

"I suppose you are about to suggest paying the good doctor a visit right now."

"Well, that is where we were headed before the detective arrived. Of course, we must also visit Louisa…"

Tom looked heavenward. "Of course, we must."

CHAPTER 25

*E*vie took in the scene, letting her eyes rest on the undulating hills and trees.

Heavens! They had pursued their suspicions and had been right all along. Martha Cooper had worked for Lord Melville. Surely, that had to mean something. Especially as he had put so much effort into denying any knowledge of her.

"It's only by entertaining even the most ludicrous possibilities that one can start asking the right questions," Evie mused. "Indeed, one should never discount asking the wrong questions, no matter how silly or farfetched they might sound."

Caro agreed. "What if? I think I will make it my habit to always ask myself that. Then again, I am hoping this will be a first and last unusual incident in this village."

Looking at Caro, Evie smiled. "Now that I think about it, Caro, you were the first to entertain the possibility of Mrs. Reid being found near the viscount's estate. And, if memory serves, I said you might be getting ahead of yourself. I believe I owe you an apology."

Their walk after lunch had given them the opportunity to absorb the news about Martha Cooper. They'd also wanted to wait for the detective to return. Since he hadn't, they decided to drive to the village and visit the doctor.

Tom had walked on ahead to prepare the motor car for their trip into the village and now stood by waiting for them.

Looking toward the house, they saw Mariah standing at a window looking at them.

"She's probably bolted the door and I'm sure the servants are all talking about me and my curious interest in investigating this death."

"I'm sure they'll only have nice things to say about you, Caro." Evie cringed. "Then again, you do have a unique insight into the way things work downstairs."

"If you are worried about the Halton House servants gossiping about you… Oh, perhaps the less you know, the better…"

"Shall we?" Tom asked.

"Yes. With any luck, we'll come across the detective. I would feel much better if he went to speak with the doctor."

Along the way, Evie said, "I can't help feeling absolved. At one point, I'd actually thought I might have been getting carried away and letting my imagination run wild. Whatever this leads to, I hope your reputation won't be tarnished."

"I suppose you're referring to our suspicions about Lord Melville."

Evie feared he would take exception to the detective questioning him again, as he was bound to do. Eventually, Lord Melville might put two and two together and realize Caro had assisted in pointing the finger of suspicion his way.

"The fact Lord Melville claimed he didn't know Martha Cooper doesn't really mean that he lied," Caro reasoned. "It could just be an honest mistake."

"Are you about to say I don't know the names of all the servants working at Halton House?"

"You are the exception. However, most people don't know all the names. Some wouldn't recognize them if they saw them in the street. Servants are supposed to be invisible."

Tom snorted.

"As I said, Evie and her household are the exception. However, in this case, Lord Melville has lost all credibility by the mere fact that he has shown an interest in the investigation."

"So, in your opinion, he acted out of character. That is genius, Caro." Being such a snob, Evie had no doubt he never noticed his servants.

Tom made the turn into the main street and pointed across the street. "That's the chauffeur. We should steer clear of him."

Evie and Caro leaned toward the passenger window and saw the chauffeur walking straight toward the pub.

"Are we curious enough to follow him?" Caro asked. "If you ask me to justify it, I won't be able to."

"Have you forgotten how aggressive he became when he encountered us on the road leading to the viscount's estate?" Tom asked. "As I said," Tom muttered, "we should steer clear off him."

"Tom, I understand your concerns, but we can't pick and choose our suspects. Following him would mean delaying our visit to the doctor, however, I am curious to know how he would react to seeing us."

"Fine, but we should keep a safe distance," Tom warned.

They climbed out of the car and took their time looking up and down the street. The chauffeur walked with purpose but they waited until he went inside the pub. The moment he did, they rushed to get there.

Instead of going inside, Tom peered through the window. "He's talking with the barkeeper and now he's settling down at a table. He brought a newspaper with him and he's reading it."

"Should we go in and observe him... from a safe distance?" Caro asked.

Tom gave a slight shake of his head. "There's no one else in the pub. We'd look too conspicuous."

Caro nudged Evie. "I can hear the roadsters coming."

Evie looked up and down the street and then saw them.

"What do we do?" Caro asked, her voice slightly panicked.

"Tom, you should stay here. You could pretend you're waiting for us and... and Caro and I will go into the store next door."

Trying to be discreet, Caro and Evie turned and walked at a casual pace.

When they entered the store, the storekeeper greeted them, "Good afternoon, ladies."

Evie and Caro glanced around and wished they had headed in the opposite direction.

"Chimney sweep and hardware store," Caro whispered.

Seeing the storekeeper rounding the counter, Evie smiled at him. "We are merely browsing."

They both sashayed toward the window and peered out. The roadsters had come to a stop outside the pub but they had missed seeing Lady McAvoy and her entourage so they couldn't be sure if they had gone inside the pub.

"How long are we going to wait?" Caro whispered. "I think the storekeeper is becoming suspicious of us."

Evie was about to say they could now step outside again when she saw the chauffeur walk by. She grabbed hold of Caro's hand and they both ducked just as he strode past the chimney sweep store.

Evie straightened. "I think the coast is clear now."

"Do you ladies require some assistance?"

They turned and saw the storekeeper standing with his hands hitched on his hips.

Caro smiled at him. "You have an interesting establishment… Everything looks very… orderly and I know you come highly recommended. I'm… I'm sure you do a fine job…"

Evie tugged Caro's sleeve and they both hurried out of the store.

"I'll never be able to go back in there again," Caro huffed. "What will he think of me?"

"Caro, I have never organized to have a chimney sweep visit Halton House. Although, in my youth, my mother made me sweep out the fireplace in my bedroom. She said she wanted to prepare me for the real world. To this day, I have no idea what she meant. Anyhow, I doubt you will ever need to go in there again."

They found Tom still standing outside the pub.

"You've missed it," he said.

"What? What happened?" They'd only been in the store for a couple of minutes.

"Lady McAvoy and her friends arrived. The moment they stepped inside the pub, the chauffeur downed his beer, got up and left."

"That's what we missed?"

"I was getting to that. He left his newspaper behind." Tom nudged his head. "Look for yourselves."

Caro and Evie stepped forward and saw Lady McAvoy and her friends sitting down, the newspaper in front of Lady McAvoy."

"Why is she patting it?" Evie asked.

"A moment ago, she removed an envelope from within the newspaper and, even from this distance, I could see it was fat with money."

"Money?" Evie's mouth gaped open. "And they found the envelope in the newspaper the chauffeur left behind? Do you think he left it on purpose?"

"That's my guess," Tom said. "Question is... Why?"

Evie turned to Caro and was not surprised to see her frowning.

"Payment for disrupting the garden party," Caro muttered. "What are we going to do about it?"

Looking around, Evie hoped to spot the detective out and about and draw his attention to a possible crime in progress.

Caro's fingers curled into tight fists. "We can't just stand here while they gloat over their ill-gotten gains."

"Caro, we can't confront them. We don't have any proof. That money could be for anything. Although…" Evie remembered the footmen had seen them meeting with, presumably, Lord Melville. "Where's the police when you need them?"

"We can't just stand here. Are you coming?" Caro didn't wait for them to answer. She stormed inside the pub and Evie and Tom had no choice but to follow.

"Let's hope Caro doesn't point her finger at Lady McAvoy. That will only prompt her to point the finger right back at Caro and then we'll have a finger pointing performance."

"Be prepared to physically remove Caro. I'm afraid she is determined," Evie warned.

Rushing inside, they entered just as Caro reached the group.

Caro slammed her hands against her hips. "You malicious little worms. I see you've received payment for your evil misdeeds."

Lady McAvoy erupted to her feet. *"How dare you?"*

To everyone's utter astonishment, Lady McAvoy took a swing at Caro who ducked just in time.

But it did not end there.

Caro growled and tackled Lady McAvoy who fell back.

"Argh! Get off me, you beast."

The others all jumped to their feet and rushed to their friend's rescue. One of the men latched on to Caro and tried to pull her away. But Tom wasted no time jumping into the fray, grabbing hold of the man's arm and pulling hard enough for him to stumble back.

That only prompted the others to draw their fists, leaving Evie with no time to think.

She joined the skirmish, pushing one woman out of the way only to be pushed herself by several people.

Evie thought she heard Caro yelp. Surrounded, Evie swung her fist and, to her surprise, it landed on a man's face.

Pain shot through Evie's hand. As she cradled it, she missed seeing a woman lunging for her. Luckily, Tom grabbed her by the waist and pulled her away.

It all came to a sudden halt when someone shouted, *"He has a gun."*

Evie's eyes widened. Grabbing hold of Caro with her uninjured hand, she pulled her back.

"Who has a gun?" Caro shrieked.

Evie swung toward the barkeeper. But he stood with his arms crossed, taking in the spectacle.

The front door swung open and two constables rushed in waving their batons.

Caro shouted, "Arrest them."

The constables rushed in and were met with the full force of resistance from the bright young things.

In the confusion, Tom snatched Evie's hand and reached for Caro before she could throw herself back into the melee.

"Let's get out of here."

As they turned, they ran straight into Detective Inspector Ian Morrow.

"Not so fast."

CHAPTER 26

At the age of ten... and a half, Evie had ambushed one of the Murphy boys by jumping from a tree she had climbed for that specific purpose.

There had been a great deal of planning and she'd practiced by swinging off a low hanging branch of the oak tree on the family farm, using a bale of hay to cushion her fall as she pictured him walking by. She had practiced timing her fall to coincide with his daily walk along the path used as a shortcut to get to the stream.

Lloyd Murphy had composed a ditty and he would sing it as he trekked along the path, the words claiming he was on his way to steal all her fish. Of course, she would have none of that, hence her determination to sabotage his plans and put an end to his thieving ways. She'd hoped he would break her fall, and he had.

Recovering from the shock, they'd both scrambled to their feet and, growling, had raised their fists...

That time, Evie had remembered to tuck her thumb.

Tom managed to convince the detective Evie's hand

and Caro's eye needed taking care of. Otherwise, they might have been subjected to a serious line of questioning by the police.

"You might want to speak with Lord Melville's chauffeur," Caro threw over her shoulder as Tom hurried them along the street.

"Does my hand look swollen?" Evie's knuckles looked quite red and her thumb throbbed.

"Did you tuck your thumb in?" Caro asked.

"I can't remember. It all happened so quickly. Heavens, I can't believe we became embroiled in a bar fight." Evie looked up from her hand and glanced at Caro. "Good grief, your eye."

"What about it?"

"It's… it's red. No, wait… there's a tinge of blue."

Caro yelped. "I saw a fist flying my way, but I thought I'd missed it."

They rounded the corner and came up to the doctor's surgery, opposite the church.

"I hope Mamma is not looking out the window. I have no idea how I'm ever going to explain this to her."

"I think that is the least of your concerns," Tom said. "I believe the detective is intent on restoring order. He might want to set an example."

They walked in and through to a small parlor which served as a reception room.

A middle-aged woman looked up. "Oh, dear." She rose to her feet and rounded the desk. "Look at your eye. You'd better sit down." The woman looked at Evie and almost took a step back. "Are you two together?"

"Yes, it's quite safe," Evie assured her.

The woman gestured to a chair next to Caro. Taking another look at her, she gushed, "Oh, heavens. You're the new Lady Evans. Oh, and you must be Lady Woodridge. I'll have to fetch the doctor. He's next door..."

As the woman rushed out of the doctor's surgery, Tom drew out a chair. "Countess, you should sit down. I can feel you shaking."

"I'm not surprised. It's not every day I take part in a brawl." Although, she thought, once upon a time, it had almost been a daily occurrence. "They were savages and merciless. I don't know what would have happened if the police hadn't arrived when they did." She'd never seen anyone react in such a violent manner. It didn't make sense, even if the money had been payment for services rendered. Evie gasped in a breath. "So, what do you think that money was for?"

Tom glanced toward the window. "Whatever it was for, they were determined to cause a distraction."

"By throwing a punch at me?" Caro exclaimed.

"I thought Lady McAvoy missed you."

"In the confusion, someone else must have landed a punch. Actually, I think I might have fallen into her fist." Caro winced. "How bad is it?"

"It's... it's always darkest before the dawn."

Caro yelped. "What does that mean?"

"I'm sure it will fade in no time." Evie looked down at her hand. "Growing up as a hoyden, I've thrown my fair share of punches. I can't believe I didn't tuck my thumb in."

They both sat back and took deep breaths.

"Tom? What did you mean by a distraction?"

He shrugged. "What's the first question you would have asked Lady McAvoy?"

"Is the money payment for disrupting Mrs. Higgins' garden party."

"Precisely. So, she caused a distraction. Like a magician. The trick is happening right before your eyes, but the magician asks you to look over there."

"Do you think she even knows why she was asked to ruin the garden party?" Evie scooped in a breath. "Assuming that's what the money was for, of course."

"Who knows? She appears to be a smart woman. Maybe she worked it out. Although, I doubt it. She hasn't been here long enough to know much about the locals."

"She's been here as long as we have and we've managed to figure out quite a few things," Evie reasoned.

"I doubt she'd be interested enough," he said. "We only became involved because Mrs. Higgins asked you to look into the missing roses."

True. Otherwise, Evie thought, they would have made a discreet exit and returned to Primrose Park.

"Follow the money trail," Evie murmured. "Tom, you said it looked like a large amount of money. Where do you think the chauffeur got it from?"

"He might have been the messenger," Caro suggested.

Tom nodded. "I'm inclined to agree with Caro."

"Does that mean we still suspect Lord Melville of seducing Martha Cooper?"

The front door opened and an elderly man walked in. He wore a dark suit, had a mop of white hair and sharp, observant eyes. They bounced from Caro to Evie and then to Tom. "I see there's nothing wrong with you." He turned to Evie and Caro. "As for you... Follow me."

Uncertain as to which one he wished to see first, Evie and Caro both stood up and followed him into a large wood paneled room with a desk in the middle and windows facing a small garden.

He walked over to a basin and washed his hands. As he dried them, he mused, "In all the years I have been tending to the good people of this village, I can't recall ever taking care of three peers in one day."

"*Three?*" Caro exclaimed.

"Lady Evans, I presume. Tilt your head up. Look to my left. My right. Up. Down. Does it hurt?"

Caro shook her head.

"You'll live." He turned to Evie. "And you must be Lady Woodridge. What is your problem?"

Evie held her hand up.

"I assume this happened at the same time as Lady Evan's black eye."

"*Black!*" Caro exclaimed.

"It's heading there." The doctor examined Evie's hand. "Did you tuck your thumb in?"

Evie looked heavenwards. "I'm sure I did. Well, no, I can't be sure. It all happened so quickly."

"Move your thumb. Up. Down. Do you often resort to fisticuffs? If you do, you should always tuck your thumb in. There's nothing broken. Does it hurt?"

Evie shook her head, although her hand did throb slightly.

"You'll live."

"Who's the third peer you tended to, Doctor?" Evie

asked.

He bandaged Evie's hand and hummed under his breath, "Someone involved in a motor car accident."

"Was it someone who crashed their motor into a farm gate?"

"I see. Word gets around quickly."

"*Martha Cooper!*" Caro exclaimed.

The doctor gave her a raised eyebrow look and asked in a deadpan tone, "Is this a recurring trait with you?"

Caro looked confused. "Pardon?"

"This is the third time you've exclaimed. Are you usually so excitable, my lady?"

"Doctor, we were on our way here to ask you about Martha Cooper," Evie explained.

"I take it you found a scuffle more entertaining."

"Pardon?"

"You said you were on your way here but you must have been diverted since you ended up with a swollen hand and Lady Evans has a black eye."

Evie shook her head. "We had intended coming straight here but, as you said, we were diverted. Anyhow, we need to find out how Martha Cooper died."

"This would be the same Martha Cooper the detective asked me about earlier today." He glanced at Caro almost as if he expected her to exclaim again.

"We are actually working with the detective. In fact, he is staying at Lady Evans' house."

"Lady Woodridge, are you suggesting that entitles you to the information or are you saying you will get the information even if I don't give it to you?" He gave her a brisk smile. "As I told the detective, Martha Cooper died in childbirth. It will be up to him whether or not he shares the rest of the information with you. Now, if you'll excuse me, I have other patients to attend to. Needless to say, you should avoid any strenuous tussles."

Stepping out of his office, Evie murmured, "That would have to be the strangest consultation I have ever had."

Caro tipped her hat down and tilted her head.

"Hold onto my arm," Evie offered as she looked up at Tom. "I suppose the detective wishes to speak with us."

"He's in no hurry, I'm sure. I just saw him driving by."

"Sedately or at high speed?" Evie asked.

"Let's just say, he drove with purpose."

Her voice hitched. "Alone or with the constables?"

"I believe the constables were with him."

"That means he's already taken care of Lady McAvoy and her entourage."

When they walked out of the doctor's surgery, Evie glanced toward the pub and saw the roadsters.

"They had better be under house arrest," Caro fumed.

When Caro took a step toward the pub, Evie stopped her. "Caro, the detective just rushed off somewhere. I'm assuming his urgency had something to do with the investigation."

"You're about to suggest we return to Primrose Park," Caro grumbled.

"If we stay, we'd only be getting in the way."

Even as Caro followed Evie to the car, she said, "You've been saying that from the start. Without our involvement, the detective would be several steps behind his investigation. We led him straight to the doctor."

"I'm not so sure about that. I don't remember mentioning the doctor."

"He would certainly never have known about Lady McAvoy and the rose murderers if we hadn't told him."

Remembering how they had avoided that particular subject, Evie grinned. "Actually, I don't think we did."

"Fine, as you say, he would have found his way to the truth eventually."

Settling in the passenger seat, Evie tried to summarize the day's events. "So, now that Martha Cooper's cause of death and place of employment have been verified, do we remain fixated on Lord Melville?"

Caro brushed her fingertip along the tender spot on her cheek. "What if…"

"Indeed. Despite Lord Melville's interest in the investigation, he has remained aloof. A guilty person would have taken action."

Evie frowned. Guilty of what? Seducing Martha Cooper and being involved in Mrs. Reid's demise?

"There is one person who has displayed unjustified aggression," Evie said.

Tom glanced over his shoulder. "The chauffeur."

Evie inspected her bandage and wondered if her hand would heal in time for their return to Halton House. "We suspected Lord Melville of seducing one of his servants but, what if?"

"What if the chauffeur seduced Martha Cooper?" Caro gasped. "It makes sense."

In more ways than one, Evie thought, although she struggled to form a complete picture.

"From the start," Caro said, "You found Lord Melville's reaction at the garden party extreme."

Yes, and she had then thought he might have used the antics to express his disapproval. Louisa's remark about him being a snob had cemented the suspicion. Evie remembered they had spoken about Mr. Higgins being in trade, something a snobbish person like Lord Melville would not approve of, especially if it involved his son marrying the daughter of someone in trade.

"*Good heavens*," Caro exclaimed. "I mean…" she lowered her voice, "good heavens. What if we are right and the chauffeur is the baby's father? And, most importantly, what if the baby turns out to be Annabelle Higgins?"

Evie nodded. "Let's assume Lord Melville knew. Of course, being such a snob, he would definitely disapprove of the match between his son and Annabelle. What if… he had planned it all?"

"Do you think the detective has reached these same conclusions?"

"I'm sure he has. We'll find out soon enough. Meanwhile, let's return to Primrose Park where we can't get into trouble."

CHAPTER 27

On the way to Primrose Park

*E*vie couldn't stop thinking about the envelope full of money. Had someone really hired Lady McAvoy to disrupt the garden party?

It seemed rather extreme to both pay for such a service and to accept money for it.

Was Lady McAvoy strapped for cash?

Would the detective consider looking into her financial situation or would he make allowances because of her title?

Caro braced herself as she exclaimed, "Good heavens."

"What?" Evie snapped out of her reverie and looked up.

A motor car was headed toward them. It appeared to be traveling at a furious pace.

Tom slowed down. She trusted him to take the necessary precautions, especially as the country road they were traveling on was quite narrow.

Caro pointed ahead. "I think there's another motor car behind it. In fact, it looks like the police motor car. Do you think they're giving chase?"

The vehicle showed no signs of slowing down. And Tom hadn't really slowed down enough to get out of its way.

At the last second, he swerved and the *ReVere* rolled into the ditch just as the other vehicle flew past them, the police car giving chase.

Tom swung around. "Is everyone all right?"

"Yes. I am." Evie looked down. "Caro?"

Caro emerged from her crouched position. "I'm fine. Did anyone see the driver?"

"The motor car looked familiar," Evie said. "I think it might have been the chauffeur, but I can't be sure."

Tom jumped out and inspected the car.

"Will you need us to get out and push?"

"We should be fine."

Caro glanced at Evie. "So much for heading home to be safe."

It took some effort, but Tom eventually had them back on the road and traveling toward Primrose Park.

When they arrived, one of the footmen emerged from the house to stand by the front door but the other one and Mariah must have been watching their arrival because the moment Caro stepped out of the motor car and looked up, they rushed out of the house.

"Milady. What happened to you?"

"No need to fuss, Mariah. We had a… slight mishap."

Five hours later...

They all sat staring at the blackboard. Caro had drawn several lines linking one name to the other until the entire blackboard resembled a messy spiderweb.

As she stepped back to make sense of it all, Mariah rushed in. "It's the detective."

In hot pursuit, the footman entered a second after Mariah and frowned at the maid, suggesting he hadn't been pleased about her doing his job.

It had been five hours since they had crossed paths with the detective out on the road.

He walked in, his shoulders slightly stooped. Before any of them thought to ask, he informed them, "We have apprehended Mr. Smithson. He's Lord Melville's chauffeur." He looked at Caro and winced but didn't say anything about her colorful eye.

"Do sit down, detective," Caro encouraged. Looking up, she asked Mariah to bring in some tea. "Or perhaps you'd like something stronger."

He declined the offer saying he could wait a while longer. "I take it you have all recovered from your near miss?" he asked.

"We haven't had time to think about it." Evie gestured to the blackboard.

"Ah, yes. I see you have been making more connections. Hush money?"

Evie nodded. "It's all we could come up with, but we don't really have an explanation."

"I suppose you're referring to the money given to Lady McAvoy." He nodded. "Due to the latest development, I managed to get Lord Melville to come down off his high horse. The money was his doing. He wanted to make sure Lady McAvoy and her friends wouldn't reveal his son's involvement in bringing them all here to disrupt the garden party."

"Frederick?" Caro exclaimed.

Evie didn't look at all surprised. "He appeared to find the garden party fiasco quite entertaining."

"You may or may not have noticed Frederick is nowhere to be seen. His father sent him away to avoid any further embarrassment." He glanced at the blackboard. "There's no mention of him."

"We found our attention constantly diverted by other suspects and people of interest," Caro said. "In fact, there are some people we meant to talk with but never got around to." She looked at Evie. "Lily will no doubt be stirring Mamma awake in the middle of the night to impart some snippet of information she forgot to mention."

Evie frowned and turned to the detective. "Are you about to suggest that is as far as Lord Melville's involvement goes?"

He studied the blackboard again. "I'm sorry to disappoint you but I'm afraid so. However..." He drew in a deep breath. "I wonder if any of this could have been avoided."

"What do you mean?"

"I suppose you are all wondering why we have taken the chauffeur into custody."

They all nodded.

"I see he's been included as a candidate for fatherhood. Well, I can confirm it. He is Annabelle's father."

They let the news sink in and then Evie asked, "Are you about to say he's also responsible for Mrs. Reid's death?"

"In a roundabout way. Knowing his employer to be an outright snob, he needed to do all he could to prevent Mrs. Reid from confronting Lord Melville."

"So, he did meet Mrs. Reid," Caro and Evie said.

"We had our suspicions and he confirmed them." He nodded. "We interviewed Lord Melville's guests. On the night of the incident, one of them was driven home by the chauffeur."

Evie remembered the detective saying Lord Melville's guests had left well after midnight, thereby providing him with an alibi. An alibi they had all found rather flimsy. "And on his return to the viscount's estate, he met Mrs. Reid."

"Yes. A purely coincidental encounter."

"Even so, what was his motive?" Evie's gaze dropped and she studied her hand.

"Are you asking or are you about to launch one of your theories?"

Evie shrugged. "I'm actually not convinced anyone killed Mrs. Reid. After all, the autopsy revealed she died from a heart attack. Have you interrogated him?"

"Yes."

Evie waited for him to say more and when he didn't,

she said, "We suspected Mrs. Reid might have been on her way to confront Lord Melville and accuse him of seducing her sister."

The detective nodded.

Evie continued, "Instead, Mrs. Reid encountered the chauffeur and he tried to stop her."

"Hence the bruises on her arms," he said.

The next question surprised him. "What about Mrs. Higgins' whereabouts twenty-five years ago? Did you manage to establish that?"

The detective sat back. "Lady Woodridge, you have left no stone unturned. In answer to your question, Mrs. Higgins spent that summer in town. She had been undergoing a medical treatment. When I spoke with her earlier this afternoon, I presented her with a scenario. One she couldn't deny. Taking a leaf from your book, I suggested she had adopted Annabelle. I'm afraid I was rather blunt and she hesitated. Before I knew what was happening, she broke down and told me the tale about her husband traveling from their country house right here in Primrose and bringing with him a baby girl." He studied her for a moment. "You're not surprised."

"Did you speak with Mrs. Higgins before or after you spoke with the doctor?"

The detective smiled. "I must admit, after my chat with the doctor, I felt rather emboldened. As you know, Mrs. Higgins' determination can be rock-solid so I was relieved to have the information at hand."

The detective filled in the details, saying the doctor had delivered the baby but hadn't been able to save the mother. Mrs. Reid had been present at the birth and had agreed it would be best to give the baby to a good family who might be able to offer her what she couldn't.

"As for the question of paternity," he continued, "Martha Cooper took that to her grave."

"How did Mrs. Reid come to suspect Lord Melville?" Caro asked.

"According to the chauffeur, Smithson, it took her some time. You see, Mrs. Reid was devastated by her sister's loss. It was only as time went by that she began to wonder. She talked herself out of suspecting Lord Melville many times because of his aloof manner. In the end, she convinced herself it couldn't have been any other man."

Evie imagined her tossing and turning and finally scrambling out of bed and thinking she needed to do something right then and there... "And she never suspected the chauffeur?" Evie asked.

"No."

"Did she know Mrs. Higgins adopted Annabelle?"

"Oh, yes, and she agreed from the start it would be best to keep it quiet."

"So, what will happen to the chauffeur now?"

He straightened. "If you remember, the autopsy provided undeniable proof of the cause of death. Mrs. Reid had a history of heart disease. Smithson had no way of knowing about her condition. He confessed to wanting to stop Mrs. Reid from confronting Lord Melville, but he insists he did not wish to harm her. I doubt this will ever see the light of day in a courtroom."

"But... What about Lord Melville's argument with

Mrs. Reid?" Evie remembered they hadn't had the opportunity to speak with Louisa's maid.

He drew out his notebook. "Yes... I asked him about that. He argued with a woman but not Mrs. Reid. The argument was about flowers she put on one of his relatives' grave. A relative he'd disapproved of, hence his burial in the churchyard instead of in the family mausoleum."

"So, in the end," Caro said, "the only murder committed was that of the roses."

"That's something to be grateful for," Evie mused. "But what about Mrs. Higgins? How does she feel about the chauffeur being her daughter's natural father?"

The detective looked down at his hands. "As to that... She doesn't know."

"You didn't tell her?"

"Brace yourself, Lady Woodridge. You're about to be surprised. Lord Melville requested my collaboration in keeping it a secret for the sake of Annabelle. He holds nothing against the young woman."

"And how does Smithson feel about that?"

"It's exactly what he wants. You see, that's why he was so desperate to stop Mrs. Reid. He didn't want any of it to come out into the open. When Martha Cooper died, he made no claim on the baby. In fact, no one knew about his relationship with Martha Cooper. He just wanted the best for his daughter and when he learned of the outcome, he could not have been more pleased. As it is, he is greatly concerned about you."

"Us?"

"He's worried you will not be able to keep this information secret. He also told me about his encounter with you and admitted to brandishing a cricket bat." The detective turned to Tom. "He's actually a sensible man and knows a cricket bat is no match for a revolver."

Caro gaped at him.

Evie remembered Tom hitching his hands on his hips. His coat would have shifted, thereby revealing his weapon.

Mariah walked in and had to wait until Caro snapped out of her state of surprise to say, "Lady Evans has sent her chauffeur with a message." Mariah handed Caro an envelope.

Caro's surprise returned. "Mamma has extended an invitation to luncheon tomorrow. She has a surprise. And the invitation is extended to you, detective."

CHAPTER 28

The next day

It seemed strange to wake up and not have an urgent purpose to pursue.

"There will be many people angry and confused about the outcome," Caro declared.

"An accidental death means there was no intention of causing harm. We'll have to accept that. In fact, as the detective claimed from the start, it was a death brought about by natural causes." However, Evie thought, the chauffeur had wanted to stop Mrs. Reid from approaching Lord Melville, hence the bruises on her arms. "I'm sure no one will demand the death sentence or even a prison sentence simply because the chauffeur tried to physically restrain Mrs. Reid. If he'd wanted to kill her, he would have had plenty of opportunities. Mrs. Reid had been visiting the village for years."

"True and a part of me feels sorry for him," Caro admitted. "All these years, he's watched his daughter from afar and he couldn't approach her to have a conversation or get to know her."

"Yes, but at least he knew she was being well taken care of."

The official statement provided by the police had closed the case. The detective had spoken with everyone who'd known Mrs. Reid and not one of them had been aware of her heart condition. Indeed, the physician who'd looked after her had been the only person who'd known about it.

"Lord Melville will not be happy about any of this," Caro declared.

"No, I can't imagine that he will." If he had been opposed to the marriage between his son and Annabelle, he would now do everything in his power to prevent it. "He will never agree to allow his son to marry the daughter of his chauffeur. I suppose he has already taken the first steps by sending Frederick away."

Checking her reflection in the hallway mirror, Evie adjusted her hat. "We shouldn't keep Tom and the detective waiting."

They stepped out into a bright, sunny day. Settling into the back seat, they made their way to Louisa's house for luncheon.

"Do you think he's carrying it now?" Caro whispered.

Evie guessed Caro meant the revolver. Studying Tom's shoulder, she couldn't see any sign of a holster. Then again, they were designed to carry the weapon and conceal the fact.

"I couldn't really say," she whispered back. "Let's not test him."

Driving through the village, they noticed the roadsters were nowhere to be seen and so they assumed Lady McAvoy had left.

"Justice has not been served," Caro muttered.

Hearing this, the detective turned. "I wouldn't necessarily say that, my lady. They have been fined for disrupting the peace. The payment they received for the havoc they caused at the garden party plus a further hefty contribution from each one has left them substantially out of pocket."

"And yet it doesn't seem to be enough."

They reached the dower house without further incident or disruptions.

Climbing out of the motor car, Caro tipped her head to one side and looked down.

"Caro, you'll trip over your own two feet. You can't possibly hope to disguise your bruise. You might as well display it with pride."

The front door opened and Lily ushered them in. "The Dowager Lady Evans is in the drawing room."

"That's odd. Lily is not usually so formal."

While they felt they could take Louisa into their confidence, they had all decided to keep the chauffeur's secret. It seemed unnecessary to risk spreading the news.

Evie considered walking in first. Instead, she stood back and herded the others in.

"Countess, is this necessary?"

"No excuses, Tom. I don't want you to be tempted by the front door."

"Ah, here you all are. Come in." Louisa stood in the middle of the drawing room wearing a shift dress with bright splashes of color.

"Louisa! That is a splendid gown."

"Thank you, my dear. It's a *Sonia Delaunay*. I picked it up in Bilbao when I last visited…" Louisa looked at Caro. "Oh, that's quite an embellishment. Lily tells me you gave as good as you got. It's a pity Lady McAvoy has already left. Otherwise, I might have been tempted to organize a soiree and give everyone the opportunity to kiss and make up." She then turned to the detective. "The triumphant keeper of the peace. It seemed you had already solved the death when the autopsy had found Mrs. Reid had suffered from a heart condition. Yet, you delved deeper and finally dug up the truth. Perhaps now you realize some things are better left undisturbed."

Evie didn't remember sharing that information with Louisa. And… it seemed Louisa had some knowledge of the events that had taken place twenty-five years before.

She looked at Caro who appeared to be equally perplexed.

"Oh," Louisa declared, "there's no great mystery. News travels. I'm sure everything we say here today will eventually be discussed at the local store tomorrow. It's strange. I actually know for a fact no one will want to spread this particular tale around. Annabelle is a sweet girl."

Louisa stepped back and that's when they all saw the reason for the luncheon invitation.

Tom blinked once and then stilled.

The detective looked surprised, intrigued and somewhat impressed.

Caro had no idea where to look, but look she did. While Evie…

Evie couldn't help herself. She burst out laughing.

"Louisa, how on earth did you manage that? I don't recall Tom sitting for you."

"Oh, heavens. I didn't really need him to sit for me. Every time I saw him, I made a mental sketch. Then, it was a matter of applying a smidgen of artistic license. What do you think? Did I do him justice?"

"Not a word, Countess. Not a word," Tom muttered.

Meanwhile…
Halton House

Millicent hadn't heard any news from Lady Henrietta and, despite keeping track of the secretary's every move, she hadn't been able to uncover anything of interest.

Peering inside a large Chinese vase, Millicent muttered, "Nothing. Not even a trace of dust." She frowned at Holmes. "You are going to cost me my position as her ladyship's maid."

She turned and glanced around the library. No one had mentioned finding the cushions.

Walking across to a table, she looked at the stack of newspapers.

The secretary had already spent the morning going through several dailies.

What could she possibly find of interest? She turned the pages, scanning them from top to bottom.

Turning another page, she noticed the bottom corner had been folded.

Scrutinizing the page, she read the headline, "Peer's daughter involved in a motor car accident." Millicent snorted. "If you ask me, she has too much leisure time on her hands."

She was about to turn the page when she noticed the article had been written by P.L.

"P.L.?" Those had been the initials on the fountain pen she'd found in the secretary's bedroom.

Excited, she searched the previous issues, going straight to the gossip pages.

P.L. was a regular contributor.

She had to tell Lady Henrietta and Toodles.

CHAPTER 29

Several days later
Halton House

"I'm glad we don't have to worry about Caro and, despite enjoying our visit, I'm glad to be home. Have you decided what you're going to do with your painting?"

"I would like to have a bonfire but I cannot bring myself to destroy the picture. I suppose it will have to live in hiding somewhere. Out of sight, out of mind. Or, we could find someone to paint clothes on *it*. I'd settle for a toga."

"I'm actually surprised you secured it so well in the roadster's dickie seat. You missed your chance to have it fly out."

"What? And have someone find it and, worse, identify me?"

An hour before, she and Tom had arrived at Halton House and had seen Henrietta and Toodles driving up just behind them.

The fact they had been hot on their heels should have triggered alarm bells...

Millicent had rushed out of the house with Holmes in her arms saying he had missed them so very much and would like nothing better than to go out for a walk with them.

Holmes had indeed been excited to see them again. Agreeing to the idea of stretching her legs after their drive from Primrose Park, they had set off for a short stroll. Then, Evie had made the mistake of setting Holmes down and the little scamp had taken off, leading her straight to the fishpond.

An hour later, bathed and changed into dry clothes, Evie walked into the drawing room.

Henrietta and Toodles studied Evie with interest. Leaning in, Henrietta whispered, "I don't really see Evangeline playing that role."

"Oh, I disagree," Toodles said. "In another life, perhaps. I think she might have made an interesting companion."

Evie eased down into a comfortable chair and slumped back. "I'm sure you want me to ask, but I simply refuse. Tom and I are thoroughly exhausted. Holmes made us chase him halfway around the estate. I had no idea his little legs could carry him so far."

Tom entered the drawing room with Holmes tucked in the crook of his arm. Looking up, he stopped. "Should I leave?"

"We've just been talking about Evie," Henrietta said.

"Evie? You mean, Evangeline."

"No, Evie." Henrietta held up a book. "We've been reading a most intriguing murder mystery and one of the characters is named Evie and she plays the role of a companion. Speaking of mysteries…" Henrietta had a whispered conversation with Toodles. "Perhaps we shouldn't say anything just yet."

If she asked, Evie knew they would both trip over each other's words in an effort to reveal their news. "I suppose this has something to do with the photographers and journalists. I didn't see any when we arrived, so I have to assume they didn't come."

Henrietta could not have looked more pleased with herself. "Yes, and you have us to thank for that."

Evie took the bait. "How so?"

"We engaged Lotte Mannering's assistance. She diverted them to Scotland and had a couple of her contacts ready and waiting to once again divert them to Ireland. Apparently, you and Tom are touring Britain and might consider accepting an invitation to sail to the Continent in a friend's yacht."

Intrigued, Evie sat up. Why had Henrietta gone to such lengths? "Oh, I see. You still haven't found a way to secure a title for Tom."

Henrietta's smile faded. "It's too early to crow. In any case, we are far too eager to hear about your trip. Don't leave out any details."

Tom made himself comfortable on a chair opposite Evie and smiled at her.

Yes, Countess, do tell them…

Evie regaled them with a version of an ideal visit to a

dear friend. She finished by saying, "So, you see, Caro, the new Lady Evans, is doing splendidly."

"Interesting." Henrietta dug inside her small handbag and produced an envelope Evie recognized and a newspaper clipping. "In one hand, I hold a letter you sent. I won't read it all but perhaps I'll refresh your memory. You described the village of Primrose as quiet and quaint."

"Oh, Henrietta, I'm sure I described it as tranquil."

"Well, on the other hand," she waved a piece of paper, "I hold a newspaper article dated a week ago. It describes the village as a warren of murder and mayhem. Which one should I believe?"

"Oh, well… I believe you have been misguided by the article. You see, there is another village with the same name." Evie shrugged. "Anyhow, I'm eager to learn what you have been doing these past few days."

Brightening, Henrietta clapped her hands. "I have been bursting to tell you. We have actually been thoroughly engaged in a mystery."

"Oh, it must be a good book."

"Book? Oh… Yes, that was rather a good book. But we have actually delved into a real mystery. We even had clues. Fountain pen. P.L. and Kensington. There's another clue but that would give it all away."

"Henrietta, I can't begin to imagine what any of that means. Is there a victim involved?"

"Not exactly, but there was some mischief."

"Was? Does that mean it has all been taken care of?" At this point, Evie began to wonder if she actually wished to hear the rest. She looked away and considered going in search of Eliza Barton, her new secretary, to find out how she had settled in.

Toodles chortled. "Since we know you won't be able to guess, we'll tell you."

Henrietta began her tale with the search for the meaning of the initials P.L. which, to her amazement, turned out to be a journalist. "He writes a gossip column and usually leads with the dramatic headline *'Peer's Daughter'*."

"Was this all part of some sort of mystery game?" The concept had really taken off recently, not just with the bright young things. Everyone seemed to be eager to figure out a mystery.

Henrietta shook her head. "No, as I said, this was real."

"And how did you come by this fountain pen?"

"Ah, well... it was found in a drawer, along with a letter."

Toodles interrupted, saying, "No, I believe the letter was found in a wardrobe, tucked between the blouses."

"Oh, yes. Anyhow, the fountain pen had belonged to P.L., the journalist. He gave it to someone as payment for services rendered and that's how it was found in that person's drawer."

"May I ask..." Evie brushed her fingertips along her forehead. "Never mind."

"You want to know precisely where these items were found." Henrietta looked quite pleased with herself. "I can't reveal that just yet. Anyhow, the letter contained a name and an address. We engaged Lotte Mannering—"

"What?" Suddenly, this all turned quite serious.

"Yes, I am still in awe of her abilities. To think, she

tackled the problem of those pesky journalists and photographers as well as this mystery. Anyhow, she followed the trail and discovered this person…"

"The one whose name you refuse to reveal?"

"Yes, anyhow, this person was meeting with P.L., the journalist. But she was a mere proxy, a go-between, acting on someone else's behalf. It turns out, this person was conveying detailed information to the journalist."

"Information? About…"

"Aha! Here is where it becomes rather interesting. You see, the person was… is related to someone you know."

Evie looked at Tom. They both shrugged.

"Yes, indeed. But you mustn't worry. We have sorted everything out."

Suddenly, it occurred to ask, "What role did Eliza Barton play in all this?" For a moment, she imagined Henrietta and Toodles conceiving a plan to help Eliza Barton dip her toes into the sort of task Evie had planned for her.

"Oh!" Henrietta nearly jumped out of her chair. "I just remembered something else. We kept Lotte Mannering rather busy. You see, when we engaged her to divert the journalists and photographers, we also asked her to look into that photograph that appeared in the New York newspaper. You will never guess. So, I will tell you." Her eyes widened. "It was all P.L.'s doing, would you believe it? We certainly had a hard time believing it. Especially as the information almost fell on our laps."

Evie remembered Caro suggesting the photographer she and Henry had engaged for their wedding might have had something to do with it.

"Did P.L. purchase the photograph from a Mr. Holmstead?" Evie asked.

"How did you know the wedding photographer's name?" Henrietta looked somewhat disappointed. "Well, I shouldn't be surprised. You were bound to get to the bottom of it. In fact, P.L. stole the photographic plates and he is now being held accountable."

"Good heavens. Eliza Barton's had a baptism by fire." Evie couldn't begin to imagine what her new secretary must have thought about Henrietta and Toodles rushing about as they must have…

Tom crossed his legs. "Perhaps we should ask Eliza Barton to come in and give us her version of events."

Evie heard a yelp.

Looking over her shoulder, she saw the drawing room door standing slightly ajar.

Had someone been eavesdropping?

Henrietta called out, "Millicent. This is your cue to come in." She gave Evie an impish smile. "We asked her to hover nearby."

Hover? Nearby? Why?

Evie's eyebrows curved up and her fingers curled around the armrest. She looked at Tom. Shrugging, he shifted in his seat and crossed his legs as if readying himself for the entertainment ahead.

Millicent entered the drawing room, her expression filled with concern.

"Milady. I trust you enjoyed your trip. How is Caro… I mean, Lady Evans?"

"There'll be plenty of time for all that later," Henrietta said. "Now, Evangeline. I want you to know what a treasure you have right here in this wonderful girl. She has single-handedly... Well, almost. She did have some help from us. Anyhow, she has proven herself to be an outstanding sleuth."

"Indeed. Do tell."

Millicent took a step back. "Lady Henrietta tells it better, milady. In fact, she really gives me too much credit."

"Oh, nonsense," Henrietta exclaimed. "Although, we did rather encourage you. Millicent, you are quite the diamond in the rough and I believe you deserve to become Evangeline's new secretary."

"My what?" Evie straightened. "Dare I ask where Eliza Barton is?"

"Oh, we sent her packing when we discovered she wormed her way into the position with the express purpose of spying on you and selling the information to P.L., yes, the journalist."

"What?" Evie slid to the edge of her chair. "Eliza Barton... a spy?"

"Evangeline, it's all worked out for the best. Millicent is only too happy to become your new secretary. And, to think, her talents might have been wasted as your lady's maid."

Did that mean she now had to hunt around for a new lady's maid?

How had this happened? She had only been away for a few days and had assumed all would be well upon her return...

"Begging your pardon, milady. I don't mean to push in, but... I will be quite happy doing both jobs."

"Evangeline?" Henrietta prompted.

"Oh, yes... And, I suppose I need to thank you for exposing a spy..."

Millicent brightened and stepped forward. "You should have seen her, milady, when Lady Henrietta sent her packing. Oh, but she was marvelous..."

Millicent, Henrietta and Toodles all talked at once, giving Evie and Tom a blow by blow account, starting with Millicent's suspicions...

∼

Later that evening

Evie removed the cap from her fountain pen and smoothed her hand across a crisp piece of writing paper.

Dear Caro,

I write to thank you for your wonderful hospitality. Tom and I were thrilled to spend time with you and look forward to many more visits.

Despite our enjoyment, as you can imagine, we were eager to return to Halton House. To our relief, we found everyone in perfect health. One does always worry, albeit, needlessly.

However, we were happy to find everything as we left it. Not a cushion out of place

. . .

Evie looked up. "That's strange." She had a habit, she rarely even acknowledged, of casting her gaze around the library and seeing familiar objects.

Closing her eyes, she saw the picture frames on the mantle and on a table. The flower vases. The paintings on the walls. The books…

She retraced her steps. There was a cushion, embroidered by Henrietta. It was always propped on a chair by the fireplace…

"I must remember to ask someone about it tomorrow."

* * * *

Printed in Great Britain
by Amazon

82181851R00150